W9-DGJ-177

SPENCER HOLST STORIES

SPENCER HOLST

HORIZON PRESS   NEW YORK

"The Typewriter Man" first appeared under the title "¢%#&?! the Typewriter Repairman" in *Mademoiselle*; "The Case of the Giant Rat of Sumatra" first appeared in *Oui*; and passages from "Pleasures of the Imagination" first appeared in *Active Anthology; America a Prophecy; Drawings by Beate Wheeler; Equal Time; Friends Seminary Review; Magazine; Prospect; Red Crow; Some/Thing;* and *Transition*.

For Beate Wheeler

CONTENTS

A Balkan Entertainment: The Man Behind the Scene

HE WAS AN operator.

He traveled frequently between Belgrade and Sofia, to Prague and Bucharest, and he was familiar with the famous, but nobody knew him.

He got things done. He arranged things. He knew criminals, he knew officials, he knew how to "fix" things. He was a specialist at covering-up the mistakes of Managers. He was a murderer and practiced extortion and acted as middleman in dealings with stolen goods.

He carried eminent credentials, but he frequently changed them. He was known to different men by different names. Though he had encountered the Soviet Secret Police many times, he baffled them. Neither the police nor public knew his nefarious part in those multifarious plots — he was always the man behind the scene.

Since his youth he had loved the sport of racing camels.

One of his more respectable roles — it was more like his hobby, a relaxation from his more deadly endeavors — was being Commissar of Camel Farms in Eastern Bulgaria on the sands; at the immense State Farm he had lavish quarters and a stable of racing camels for his private use, and a swimming pool. His butlers were bodyguards. His accountants were forgers, and they kept the books at the farm impeccably — the place always showed a profit — so that his superiors in Sofia never had cause to investigate him, or to question the way he ran the place. And he was truly proud of his animals who frequently won prizes in foreign fairs in Turkey, Egypt, Arabia and India, and abroad brought the Motherland much admiration.

9

It would be a slur to suggest that thieves in Communist countries are less intelligent or less successful than their American or European counterparts. As many shops are robbed in Moscow as in New York, Soviet safecrackers are as "cool with their soup," as many priceless paintings vanish from their museums, Soviet embezzlers are not less daring, vast frauds are successfully perpetrated — but these dramatic events are not reported in the daily press, or the popular magazines.

His fingers were in many pies filled with the fruits of crime.

He had connections everywhere and if there was anything he knew how to do it was how to pull strings, to force people to do things, as often as not, things they'd never dream of doing.

So that when he sent out invitations to twenty very prominent individuals to come to the farm on a summer afternoon to witness a demonstration of camel-riding like they'd never seen before, those people came.

They came in limousines. They flew in from Moscow, and some from Warsaw and East Berlin. The premier of Yugoslavia came accompanied by his country's finance minister, and they looked vexed and pale, their eyes protruding wildly as if they had not slept. A very holy man, the Patriarch of Constantinople, flew in from Istanbul with a look of hope on his face. A Chinese magician was there, a man revered by professional conjurors and stage magicians, and famous for his animal illusions. An eminent physicist came from Siberia. The museums of the Soviet were well-represented, an elegant, bespectacled bunch. There was also a giant baboon on a chain, but it is uncertain where he came from or what he represented, but by his side stood the crackerjack reporter from Pravda, talking to the man from Tass and the senior editor of Izvestia.

There they all were on the dot at Noon at the start of a

straight fifty-yard racetrack. This is the traditional length and shape of the camel-racing track. On the track itself was a huge table.

With athletic grace the operator leaped atop the table and addressed the notables, saying, "Gentlemen, I have invited you here to witness a demonstration of camel-riding. I am going to ride a camel once down this track and I want you to watch me. Of all my accomplishments I am most proud of the way I ride. All my life I've been the man behind the scene, but recently I've discovered that at heart I am a show-off. After today I shall never again engage in behind-the-scenes activity. Today you will witness that I change my way of life. Today I shall be a show-off."

"First I shall show you my wealth (I am a multimillionaire) and the rare objects I have come to possess. And I make you a bargain! If I put these things into your hands — then you must not be overwhelmed, then for five minutes you must turn away from these treasures, then you must watch me ride! After that you may do what you will with what you see. . . ."

And out walked what was probably the prettiest camel in the whole world.

Undoubtedly it was the prettiest camel in Bulgaria. It was led to the table and the notables noted that it was cleverly laden with bundles. In a moment attendants unloaded the camel, spreading out boxes, briefcases and unusual objects along the table. The attendants opened the boxes and half-spilled their contents of cash, gold, and jewels onto the table.

Strangely, it was the most timid man in that whole group who was the first to speak. He was chief of the rare manuscripts division of the Leningrad Library, he had found a manuscript on the table, and once he started talking there was no stopping him — "His lost play! His last play! The only copy! Look! Printed out in capitals and underlined twice, it says —

FINAL SCRIPT
(corrected by the author)

"And it's signed William Shakespear!" shouted the librarian, wagging the manuscript in the air. "Look at the way he spells his name! Look at the way he spells his name! Twenty years ago it was found in the stacks and that afternoon scholars pronounced it genuine, but by evening it had vanished. (We were warned by the authorities never to speak of it, the theft was hushed up.) But this is that manuscript! Look everyone! The front page bears the stamp of the Leningrad Library! This is our book and it's been kept out too long, this play is long overdue . . . why the first performance of Shakespear's last play shall be given in Moscow! Then perhaps it could be taken to London . . . and later to New York . . . for this play belongs to the whole world!

"But this manuscript," he added, "belongs to the Leningrad Library."

The truth is that no one there heard a word this man had said, for each had found something separate on which to rivet his attention.

The museum fellows each had found a long-lost painting, and had anyone been listening, they might have been heard to whisper, each to each, "Our van Eyck! — Our Vermeer! — Our Velasquez! — Our Monet!"

Another whispered, "The Treasures of Troy!"

The premier and his finance minister found a bulky briefcase, took one look in it and snapped it shut, and each got a grip on the handle and stared hard into the eyes of the other. The bag contained practically the whole treasury of Yugoslavia in foreign negotiable securities.

But of all the objects on the table it is possible that the most valued was the splinter of wood about three inches long at which the Patriarch stared, startled and awe-struck. He moved toward the table so cautiously, so quietly, yet with such intensity, such was his curiosity, that the whole group finally turned to watch him, hand outstretched, hesitate to touch the splinter. It was just an old piece of wood, but it looked very, very old.

The old man touched the fragment of wood and he smiled.

Everybody saw it — his face radiated happiness.

Whatever it was the old man hoped to find there, he had found it.

He looked up at the operator who was still standing on the table and he asked, "What *else* can you show us?"

"*This!*" answered the operator, and he held between two fingers a tiny object, brilliant lemon-yellow and strangely shaped. "We must now go to the other end of the racetrack," he told them. "You will be better able to view me riding my camel from there."

The operator leaped off the table and took a few steps toward three open limousines, and the chauffeurs started the motors.

"But what is that you have in your hand?" several of them asked. Obviously none of them knew what it was.

But the Patriarch said, "Young man . . . is that object in your hand something used in the game of golf? Is that not, in fact, a golf tee?"

"Golf? Golf? What is that?" asked those eminent men of one another. That golf tee mystified them, and fascinated them, for you understand, there is not a single golf course in the whole of the Soviet Union.

"Follow me," said the operator holding the golf tee aloft so that they could all see it. "And leave my things there on the table. After you watch me ride, then you can do what you will with all that you see."

The group entered the limousines and were driven to the other end of the track to the finish line.

"Notice," said the operator, "that a tiny hole has been

drilled down through the center of the golf tee, and now look at this."

He held in his other hand a short darning needle, and he dropped it into the hole so that the eye of the needle protruded over the top of the tee. And from a chauffeur he procured two magnifying glasses which he presented to the magician and the physicist.

"Would you kindly assist me," he asked them. "Would you examine this needle, especially the inside of the eye, and notice that it is clean, and unmarked." They did this. And after pressing the golf tee into the ground on the racetrack's finish line so that the top of the tee was just level with the surface of the track, he told the two, "When I finish my ride, without touching the needle, would you please examine it again."

And now he addressed them all. "You may wonder why I became a millionaire in the Soviet Union. If you ask a mountain climber why he climbs a mountain, he will answer: Because it is there, because it is possible. And that is why a criminal becomes a millionaire, because it is possible, that is all. And now I shall ride . . . Drive me to the start of the track!" he directed a chauffeur, and he stepped onto the running board of a limousine and was driven back to where the camel stood.

From where they stood the spectators could see to their dismay that the attendants had put all the treasures back into the bundles and that the bundles were being thrown onto the camel.

The operator leaped onto the camel and held his arms out wide. Two attendants thrust into his hands two huge paint brushes, and two more attendants held up two huge bowls filled with vermilion paint. He thrust the brushes into the bowls and swirled them around in the paint, and then shouted, "Go!"

Holding the brushes, his arms stretched wide, he rode with the reins in his teeth.

14

The camel got halfway down the track before the spectators noticed that unlike most objects as they approach us, the camel and its rider did not appear to be getting any larger. Indeed, by the time they were three-quarters of the way down the track it was quite clear that the camel was no larger than a Great Dane and the man was perhaps the size of a monkey. By the time they were five yards from the golf tee the camel had shrunk to the size of a cat and the man was no bigger than a mouse. When last seen — a few feet in front of the tee — they were no bigger than an egg. And then they vanished, treasure and all.

The spectators looked at one another, while the magician and the physicist bent to examine the needle with their magnifying glasses. On the inside of the eye of the needle — one on either side — they found two dots of vermilion paint.

*   *

"I don't see why I was invited here," said the magician. "This was no stage trick."

"I don't understand why I was invited here," said the physicist. "This hocus-pocus is nothing a scientist would understand."

"I am sure what we saw was no hoax," said the Patriarch. "However, I feel I would be personally damned were I to proclaim it a miracle."

And the premier said that he would be damned if he was going to reveal that he had witnessed the entire treasury of Yugoslavia being stolen by a thief who rode off on a camel through the eye of a needle.

And it would soon be discovered that there were no camels at all on the farm, that during the previous month the men who worked here had taken all the camels abroad, never to be heard from again — *the man had stolen every camel in Bulgaria!*

Not a line has been published about it, and there is no record anywhere of this occurrence. Those men took a vow never to reveal even to their most intimate colleagues what they had seen with their own eyes. The whole thing was hushed up.

But of course they told their wives.

This report is merely the gossip of Belgrade.

If it had happened in America — where they publish everything — it would have been a different story.

The Case of the Giant Rat of Sumatra

A JAR OF OLIVES in pitch darkness on the shelf of the restaurant kitchen in the small hours of the morning . . . the place closed and everyone gone. . . .

A large rat, fat and round as an olive, sat on its haunches on top of the jar.

It sniffed intently, and listened to the shrieking wind blowing a blinding blizzard into huge drifts. A 50-mile-an-hour wind in fifteen-below-zero weather boded death for the Traveler, and made even the restaurant kitchen unusually chilly, the water pipes having frozen, and there was ice in the sink.

High North Atlantic tides and the weather had forced the huge wharf rat to abandon its usual haunts — its nest was soaking wet — and seek shelter in this kitchen. He was a ten-year-old male from Sumatra three months off the ship from Rangoon and it was his first experience of the Norwegian winter.

He sat on the olive jar and twitched his whiskers, and listened long, for surrounding him and coming at him from every direction was the odor of . . . cat. Two cats guarded this kitchen. For an hour the rat sat there in the dark, relatively warm, waiting quietly, and the rat heard no sound . . . except the wind, and in the distance the sloshing surf that had flooded his nest in the warehouse that faced the fjord.

A number of hours later the owner of the restaurant with his wife entered the building. They discovered the kitchen in chaos, evidence that a fantastic fight had taken place, blood all over the place, and small bones in the middle of the floor that had been eaten clean.

"What's wrong with this cat?" asked the wife who had found one of her cats huddled in a dark corner trembling and mewing softly, whimpering in a state of shock. The old lady sensed that the cat was not even aware of her presence. "What could have frightened her so?" inquired the old lady.

"Whatever it was," answered her husband, kneeling and examining the pile of bones, "it ate the other cat."

2

Large tropical wharf rats are noted for their uncanny intelligence, there are many stories of a fabled cleverness at avoiding traps, and this rat was quite bright.

During his entire stay in Norway he was not seen by a single human being.

And one is tempted to assume it was his wharf-rat intelligence that caused him soon to climb a cable of a ship about to set to sea, no doubt with a notion to return to Sumatra and warm sunshine.

The rat obviously couldn't understand Norwegian or he would have heard the sailors talking, and known that this ship — it was the ill-fated *Matilda Briggs* — housed an Arctic expedition.

Shortly thereafter the ship entered the pack ice, the ship became frozen in the ice, and the men huddled in the icy boat barely clinging to life as hopeless months passed and their provisions eventually gave out.

The rat's whiskers quivered with cold, and his eyebrows froze.

The leader of the expedition with three others set off on foot across the pack ice with the intention of bringing back help for those who stayed inside the meager shelter of the ship; and of course they succeeded, they brought back help, and a number of those who had waited, suffering in the ship, survived.

Among those who survived was an old English seaman, not an officer or anything — an old salt. On his first day in a civilized port, as he sat in a fancy tavern eating kidney pie, he was interviewed by an English journalist, a lady.

"Did the men pray?" asked the journalist.

"God *answered* my prayer!" said the seaman seriously. "It was a bloody miracle . . . about the rat!"

"What do you mean?" asked the journalist.

"There was a tropical wharf rat aboard, and I was determined to catch it. Many, many months I tried. I'm handy with tools, and I built a half-a-dozen traps, each more ingenious than the last. The men said I was mad, they said I was obsessed with catching the rat . . . but in the end they admitted I wasn't crazy. You see, it saved our lives. I'll never forget it was in the middle of an endless night, the party had left on foot four months before . . . finally in desperation I got up on the kitchen table so that the other sailors could see me, and I kneeled and clasped my hands, and I said out loud so that all could hear — I prayed to God that I catch the rat. And at that moment . . . so that all could hear it, there was a loud click, the sound of my trap snapping shut. I had caught the rat alive. If ever there was one of God's creatures who was at the right place at the right time, it was that rat in my trap. After that we all knew that God was with us, was with us in the very room."

"You caught the rat . . . I see . . ." said the bewildered lady. And then she added, frowning heavily, "But what did you do with the rat?"

"We ate it," said the seaman. "Tasted like Chinese food. He was a remarkably healthy animal. Can't figure out what he ever found to eat on the ship, but he was round and fat as an olive."

"Did you like the taste?" asked the lady.

He looked sharply at her, for how could she know how many traps he had contrived, what a battle of wits it had become, the wharf-rat intelligence at avoiding traps pitted against the human intelligence of the animal trapper. But the trapper, the human, had finally won out; after many months in an endless night the human brain surpassed the wharf-rat brain . . . with a little help from God . . . and how could this poor lady understand that satisfaction? Grinning broadly he said, "Like Chinese food — it was delicious!"

3

Yet what does an old sailor know of the world?

What can he know of the life of the English journalist? Would it surprise him that a journalist would think nothing of eating a few mice on an afternoon?

Let us follow this lady as she leaves the restaurant and notice how, at the nearest garbage can, she disposes of her notes, and now as she enters a rather shabby deserted street along the waterfront she removes her pearls and rings, throwing these, along with her pocketbook, into another refuse can. Now her journey takes an unexpected turn as she slips between two abandoned buildings, and in those darkest shadows — is she taking off her clothes?

Now out of those darkest shadows comes a cat.

A skinny tomcat all sinew and bone.

He pauses a moment and goes beneath a fence and now down deserted passageways, now through a broken basement window into what some might call a cozy apartment, though somewhat messy, and smelling strongly of pipe tobacco and chemicals.

A rather large, comfortable old gray cat who had been

napping, stirred and said, "Eh! What! Is that you Holmes? Where the devil have you been?"

"Watson, my good fellow! Don't bother getting up! I've been disguised as a lady journalist and I've had an enlightening conversation with a sailor, and he told me everything I wanted to know. Watson, do you recall several years ago in a Norwegian port there was a brutal murder and that I said I would not rest until I knew the fiend had gotten his just deserts?"

"You mean the waterfront restaurant murder! Two cats, sisters, I believe . . . lived alone in the restaurant. One found brutally murdered, and *eaten*, and the other left a raving lunatic! A hideous business!"

"And do you recall, Watson, that I found at the scene of the crime a hair from a large wharf rat that had lived in Sumatra and come to Norway via a ship from Rangoon. I learned that here in my laboratory from studying the hair. I could find no witness, neither cat nor human, who had seen such a rat in the vicinity. Yet I knew he had been there, and after awhile I realised he had escaped. I studied the shipping lists and the only boat he could have left on was the *Matilda Briggs*, Arctic bound. Well at long last, Watson, the ship has returned, and today I got positive proof that a rat fitting that description was indeed aboard, and was caught alive, and then eaten by the crew. So though no one in Norway ever once laid eyes on the murderer, even so, he is discovered and dead; he got his just deserts. Justice was served. I think we can call that case closed."

4

The gray cat fumbled with a key held awkwardly in his paw trying to open his desk.

"Watson, allow me to assist you with that," said Holmes, easily opening the recalcitrant drawer which held the famous files kept by Dr. Watson on the cases of Sherlock Holmes. "Watson, sometimes I think you're ambisinistrous," chided the great detective.

Watson blushed. "I was thinking of something else! Damnation about the key — I had an idea! The title! Imagine this in large letters in my Table of Contents: The Case of the GIANT RAT OF SUMATRA . . . What do you think?"

"Watson, old friend, the world is not ready for this tale. You must not publish it."

"What's that you say! Not publish it! Tosh! Certainly I'll publish it, it's one of your greatest triumphs!"

"Confound it, Watson! Don't you see? You'll be revealing the Secret of Literature, and the world isn't ready for it, especially the publishing world isn't ready for the Secret of Literature. There is no way you can tell the story without revealing that you and I are Conan Doyle's cats. When an author's cat wishes to dress-up and act like a man he becomes a character in a book, and in fiction no one can discern that we are not regular people. But it must remain secret! The publishing world — those editors, those critics, those literary agents of whom I know you are so fond — would be dismayed, Watson, *deeply* dismayed to learn you are a cat, that Lady Chatterley, Bloom, Scrooge, Robinson Crusoe, and Moby Dick himself were all cats! Cats all! And your friends . . . unquestionably . . . would grow to feel queer about their work. . . ."

"Good Doctor Watson, don't you see? The Case of the GIANT RAT OF SUMATRA must never be published . . . ever. I, Sherlock Holmes, forbid it!"

The Frog

A FROG THAT BECAME addicted to morphine during experiments at the Federal hospital at Lexington, Kentucky, fell into my hands at the conclusion of their experiments. As a frog, he was a wreck. Unless he had morphine he wouldn't eat or even look at a fly. I kept him as a pet and gave him a name, but it became rather a problem supplying him with morphine. Being merely a laboratory assistant and not a doctor or even a nurse I had no access to the drug which many doctors here are studying, attempting to discover a cure for human addicts.

However I'd gotten to like him. He was a full-grown bullfrog, slimy and green, and I kept him in a fishtank cage in my room which was on the grounds of the hospital in a building occupied by laboratory assistants, nurses aides and kitchen workers. All the fellows on the floor became fond of his voice. Ordinarily I believe frogs croak only in the evening but our frog would begin to croak whenever he needed a fix. It was a mellow beautiful belch, mellifluous, euphonious, and strong, and I might add, very male, not as loud, but not unlike the bellow of a bull from a hilltop.

I'd been to the dentist several months previously and I had some pills for pain which I had never used, stuck away in my dresser drawer. I crushed them and added a little bit to his water and he gulped it right down and was quiet. Because a frog doesn't weigh much it doesn't take very much of an opiate to be effective, and, by careful division of the dosage, the white powder I had made from my pills lasted several weeks.

A baker from the hospital kitchen whose room was down the hall from mine next furnished me with some cough medicine which had been prescribed for a throat infection. Actually he shared the medicine with the frog every day, depriving himself so the frog wouldn't get sick. But the baker got well, his hacking cough abated, and my frog was out of opiate again.

He croaked all night.

I wasn't sleeping myself, and about 3 a.m. I heard a slight noise outside my door and as I glanced in that direction, saw a white envelope being slid under my door. I got out of bed and

22

opened the door, but whoever had done it had vanished. Inside the envelope was — Lord knows what it really was, perhaps it was actually heroin, but more probably it was medicine someone had snitched from one of the wards. Anyway, it worked. I put a tiny fraction of it in his water and he gulped it eagerly, and then stared at me with a long grateful look. The pupils of his eyes were like pinpoints. Soon he closed his eyes and rested contentedly, though I doubt he slept. But everyone on our floor finally did.

He was a swell frog.

Everyone on the floor was familiar with his medical history and was discreet about his problem for otherwise I think I might have gotten into trouble if any of the staff nurses or doctors had discovered what I was doing.

Only men lived in our building but on weekend afternoons we were allowed to have female visitors in our rooms and frequently these guests were brought in to meet my frog.

He was our mascot.

One afternoon a laboratory assistant with whom I often worked, and who was a friend, was visited by his two teenage sisters, and he brought them into my room. They made a big fuss over the frog and one of them insisted on holding it in her hands. She was a terribly pretty young thing. She didn't mind that it was wet and she insisted on giving him some medicine herself. The frog was quite content and seemed almost especially friendly. He sat there in her hands as if he liked it.

I had left the room for a minute, leaving the two girls and my friend and the frog in my room, when suddenly I heard what sounded like a peal of thunder and a brilliant light flooded the hallway, emitted from my room. I rushed into the room and saw a stranger standing there, a tall Italian-looking guy.

"What happened? And what are you doing in my room?" I demanded of the stranger. I gave a quick glance at the scene and added, "And what happened to my frog?"

The girl answered, "I kissed the frog — and this man appeared in a big flash of light."

"Allow me to introduce myself," volunteered the stranger to the girl. "I am Prince . . . . " and he rattled off some Italian name which I couldn't make out. He continued, "Many years ago I was transformed into a frog, to remain one until I should be kissed by a maiden. My dear, will you become my wife? I know where there is a great treasure, and you shall live in a palace, among beautiful fountains and great old trees where the weather is always like summer. Will you be my wife?"

The sweet child's lip curled into a sneer, and her eyes opened wide with astonishment. She answered, "You think I would marry a junkie? Never!"

"In that case, my friends, I bid you good day. My best wishes to you all — goodby forever." And so saying he stepped out the window, and I never saw him again.

I have since decided he was a burglar and that he stole my frog, because I never saw my frog again either.

It is true however that a couple of years later my friend, the laboratory assistant with whom I often work, showed me a picture on the society page of a New York newspaper. He said, "Look! There's that burglar who stole your frog!"

It is true there was a remarkable resemblance. It was a photograph of a princess of the Netherlands with an Italian prince, and they were soon to be married.

But you know how newspaper photographs are.

I don't think it was the same person.

I told my brother-in-law not to mention it because my wife likes to kid me about how she might have married a prince, and so I didn't even bother showing her that photograph.

Finders
Keepers

THE NEATLY DRESSED immigrant family who died in five days of different diseases from picking through piles at the city dump for the bag of cash that had got into the garbage — I'll never forget the industriousness of that family, for while they searched through bags of filth for their life savings, I came to watch them. I am their garbageman.

The first day I came I brought the cash.

But allow me to explain: I work with two other men on a garbage truck. One is the driver, and the other, like me, empties the cans into the rear of the truck. On this particular day as I threw out the contents of a can I noticed a brown paper bag that had money in it. My partner was across the street so I stuffed the bag inside my shirt and didn't say anything. I was at home by noon that day and discovered thirty-eight thousand dollars was what I had.

That evening the newspapers were full of it. The man had wanted to purchase a house for cash and had taken every cent out of his savings account. The man had nine children. There were photographs of him weeping. Somehow the money had gotten thrown out with the garbage and it wasn't discovered until after the truck had been unloaded. The driver knew exactly where he had dumped his load, but the trouble was that two other trucks had discharged the day's refuse in the same place, on top of the load that should have had the money in it. It was a mess.

The police cordoned off the area where they thought the money might be with bright blue rope. And that night a city fire truck illuminated the scene with powerful lights, so that the family could search through the day's refuse of a city. Throngs of spectators, informed through the radio and press of the family's plight, came to watch. Many, many offered to help. But the distraught man who had lost his money indignantly, you might say hysterically, refused all help, and he pleaded with the police to keep the crowd outside the blue rope. He would allow no one except his family to search for the money, and a thoughtful police captain, after surveying the scene and after a consultation with the mayor, decided to allow the man his way, and indeed to help him in what ways they could in his search for the money. Television crews added their lights to the ghastly scene which they reported on the morning news; and the next day the whole city was waiting for the money to be found.

I report here that I didn't sleep well that night.

Earlier I had been interviewed several times by the police, and by my supervisor, and without question they believed me, for I have worked for the sanitation department for ten years.

I am still amazed at how easily I lied about it, but then no one from the beginning ever suspected me. They dismissed my words as being the truth, and turned their attention to the monstrous mound of garbage.

Ordinarily the garbage would have been plowed and treated with chemicals but now they let it lie there untreated and soon a noxious odor flooded the vicinity. I don't see how all those people could stand it. It was a strange crowd, those who came to watch, and there were several scuffles with the police that night with irate citizens who insisted it was their Right to search for the money. They argued that if the money had been thrown into the garbage and the garbage delivered to the city dump — that it was now public property, and that it was everybody's right to search for it, and that whoever found it should be allowed to keep it.

You might think I would agree with that logic, but the truth is I didn't. If the man had thrown away the money it would have been a different story, but he had merely by accident misplaced it, and the money was obviously still his.

As I regularly do I went to work quite early in the morning the next day, and on returning home, having taken a shower and had a hot soak, as I always do after work, I sat and watched the Noon News while having a bite to eat. I remember I was eating a tuna fish sandwich.

There I saw the noon wrap-up of the night's garbage scene.

I saw the three people whom the police had arrested being hauled away in police vans. There was a garrulous, wild old woman who shrieked at the cameras, and a strange, prissy college student who threw himself on the garbage heap and went rigid so that it took three plainclothesmen to carry him off, and another, a middle-aged man who looked dangerous, like a huge rat, like a man who obviously belonged in jail, who regularly drank too much, was handcuffed and hustled into a patrol car.

These were those who passionately believed in finders-keepers.

I decided to return the money.

I put the package of money in my lunch bucket, and took the bus to the end of the line where the city dump was located, where there must have been two hundred people milling around.

It was easy to find the family. They had set up two tents just inside the blue rope where they took turns napping, while the others searched.

And there they were, that neatly dressed family, kids of all sizes, on the garbage heap.

I had been picking up their garbage for five years, three times a week, and the whole family had become quite familiar to me. I had noticed how the children grew, and occasionally, though not often, I had had brief conversations with them, giving them information about our pick-up schedules. Indeed, among all those strangers they seemed like old friends, and I went directly to the man, who was inside the blue rope, to give him his money. He saw me approaching, but I could see he didn't recognize me. He rose to his feet and frowned oddly at me, thrusting his jaw out at the same time.

Then incredibly he twisted his body into a strange posture like a dancer and his leg shot out like a fist and his heel hit my stomach, so that I fell back outside the blue rope, doubled-up with pain. He shook his fist at the crowd around me, and then bent again to search through the garbage.

It was several minutes before I could speak, and then some stranger helped me to my feet. Shakily I stumbled back toward the bus stop, away from the mob of onlookers who had witnessed the encounter. As I fled, I heard someone shout, "Hey buddy! Is this your lunch bucket?" I thanked the stranger.

The Largest Wave in the World

A HURRICANE SENT THE 200-foot radio tower dancing upright across the fields, its guide wires trailing giant blue sparks.

The suspension bridge split lengthwise down the middle. Each side of the highway was suspended by vertical strands to its single cable, and though the two great cables stayed firmly fixed to the towers, the two pieces of highway broke loose and were pushed mightily away from the towers and flapped horrendously in the great winds. Built of massive blocks of stone and steel sunk deep into bedrock the bridgetowers held firmly to the ground, but the tops of the towers began to

28

vibrate like two buzzers, or more precisely: as the towers were sunk into a single great piece of stone, and as the towers themselves were perfect geometric replicas of each other, the bridgetowers buzzed in phase like the prongs of a tuning fork, producing a single pure tone. For fifteen minutes while the eye of the storm passed overhead, the buzzing resonated inside that giant cylinder of still air, and a strange musical tone was heard around the world.

Every seismograph jammed, and it's judged that it was the loudest continuous sound heard on earth during the time since life began.

In the base of the bridge tower, deep inside, were a number of rooms where a hundred people huddled in more or less comfort, safe from the holocaustal winds. As the eye of the storm passed overhead, and as the wind suddenly died down to an uncanny dead calm, those people ventured outside to look around in wonderment. This bridge is located on the Eastern coast of the United States and the bridge crosses a wide river just before the river empties into the Atlantic Ocean. When those hundred people came outside onto a broad stone terrace they looked out toward the nearby ocean, and saw the sea hugely tossing though there was not a breath of wind, and they noticed an odd silence.

Some shouted at the top of their lungs and one raised a wooden chair into the air and crashed it to the floor, but those activities made not the slightest sound.

For the strange musical tone had "jammed" their ears, just as it jammed the seismographs. Their ears temporarily had stopped functioning. They were utterly deaf. Later they all said they could hear the mysterious musical note, not with their ears, but with every cell in their bodies.

After several minutes had passed they noticed that the waters of the ocean were receding. Where a moment before the waters had been hugely tossing it was now dry land, and that place where the water met the land now seemed several miles away. The thick billows of clouds of the hurricane wall rose thirty thousand feet into the early evening sky and came down to a hundred feet above the surface of the ocean; but as now the level of the ocean fell, the clouds retained their altitude, so soon they had a view beneath the storm of the floor of the ocean which was now dry land as far as they could see; and in the far distance they all say they saw a range of mountains though no islands rise above the surface in that direction; and they say they saw between two mountain peaks a brilliant orange moon, *they insist they saw the moonrise*, that it bathed them in orange light, and that the whole bridge was bathed in orange light. And that it took several minutes before the glowing moon slipped up behind that whirling wall of cloud that by then was fast approaching. In sudden pitch darkness and wind they scrambled into the rooms at the base of the tower, and locked the doors tight.

And every one of those people survived it, the wave.

The Lovers

ONCE UPON A time a forest boy fell flat on his face.

The boy was a wild thing, lost by his parents in the Amazon maze of animal paths and rivers which border the million islands of mystery, those places where man has never touched his foot, unexplored places where dangers or treasures lurk, or nothing.

Where only animals roam, and exceptions, explorers, occasionally.

His parents had not been exceptions. They were missionaries and had stuck to the rivers, to their canoes with their Indians who were taking them to a distant village inside

Brazil where there was civilization of a sort, but no Christians. A village of mud huts where ignorance reigned, where rituals took the place of medicine, and on Saturday nights hallucinations from a green plant took the place of movies.

The boy, who was five then, climbed on a log in the night and pushed it into the river and floated away.

He was scared.

He looked up — and there was the man in the moon smiling down at him. He smiled back, and waved.

The many-forked river swallowed him in its mystery, and the search for him was fruitless.

They assumed he was dead.

He was having a wonderful time!

He had stolen a knife from one of the Indians, and he cut fruit from overhanging trees as he glided past, and lunched on the abundance of the jungle.

With his parents he'd been terrified.

But away from them, free, he felt no terror of anything. He scampered about petting pythons, black panthers, playing with hairy spiders, sporting bravery as other children wear lead police badges over their hearts, with nonchalance and happiness at the glitter of it in the sunshine.

He swam in alligator pools and his absence of fear, coupled with coincidence, time after time protected him.

He loved everything and everything loved him back — and amused him, and fed him, and was a pillow and his blanket that, unspeaking, cared for him.

He wandered, and swung on the vines from the trees, and swam, and made spears, all for the fun of it, until he was sixteen, until the day at that time, he fell flat on his face.

He fell in love.

He was flying through the air on a vine, wrapped in a skin he'd cut from an old jaguar corpse he'd found, as he crashed into a parrot flying.

They both fell.

The parrot had broken its wing, and was skwaaaking and running in circles hysterically. The boy chased it and caught it in his arms.

The parrot bit him.

The boy carried him at arm's length until he reached a rude hut he'd built. He blocked the door and let him go.

But instead of trying to escape the parrot collapsed.

The boy wondered what to do, so he went over and began to stroke him, and he laid him in a bed of leaves, and sprinkled water on him.

The parrot was breathing. He went for food.

He climbed a clakatee tree and gathered white nuts which hung from long strings, which he knew parrots liked the best, for these trees were filled with them every morning. On mornings past he had watched the parrots cover the tree with their rainbow bodies, skwaaaking excitedly as the sun rose, devouring the nuts.

He laid the food beside the parrot and sat watching.

He straightened his feathers and petted him some more.

The next day the parrot revived a little and ate a little and hobbled across the hut into a dark corner.

He stayed there all the while his wing was healing; the boy fed him, and brought him water; the parrot got well, that is, he lived, but lost the use of his wing.

He loved this parrot as he would have loved a girl, had there been a girl in the jungle.

The parrot also fell in love in the only way a parrot can — he allowed himself to be tamed.

They lived together.

They traveled together — the boy flying through the trees, swinging from vine to vine through the air, while the parrot ran like a mad chicken on the ground.

He taught the bird to talk, to laugh, to cry, to say hello —

goodby, to use the language he had almost forgotten from lack of use, due to his separateness from human beings.

Some years they lived together — until, indeed, the boy became a man of twenty five. He had grown short, his body was blackened by exposure to the wind and sun, his hair hung in beautiful bleached golden snarls down to his waist, and his eyes flashed like an animal's with gentleness.

He wore a leather thong tied tightly around his waist, through which was stuck the dagger he'd stolen years ago, the only possession he valued.

And the only thing he valued more was his love.

They always slept together, the parrot perched on a stick, over the man, as if guarding him. Every night the man would say — Happy dreams.

And the parrot would repeat in his skwaaaking voice — Happy dreams.

When he walked the parrot would often sit on his shoulder repeating phrases like a broken record.

He still knew no danger, never felt fear, was friendly with all the animals. He was gentle as a dandelion.

His wanderings over the jungle were aimless and one day he saw smoke over a hill from a trading post. He approached curiously, but suddenly stopped. Dead still.

There was a thrashing sound in the undergrowth ahead and he heard a woman's voice say — Tie my boot, dear. It keeps coming undone. Here. Let me hold your gun. . . .

The first human voice he'd heard in twenty years stabbed, like an ice pick, his stomach, stirred memories, and he dropped to the ground behind a big bush.

That voice.

Impossible.

It sounded like his mother.

Was it really his mother?

Were they still looking for him?

The parrot, not knowing all people were not like his master, scrambled through the foliage at the voice.

The woman screamed.

Bang!

The parrot shrieked.

He dashed through the brush and caught the parrot's last words — Happy dreams!

He turned to the woman holding the smoking rifle, and the man at her side.

His eyes were like forest fires.

He leaped at the woman, but the man grabbed his gun, and it smoked, and he fell with a pain and hole in his stomach.

Confused, his stomach burning, he stared at them. They stared back, just as amazed.

He jumped again — at the man — and took a bite from his throat.

Then he raced through the jungle, through the trees, clutching vines, jumping, falling from branch to branch. Away! Away! He must get away and he went, scrambling and howling like the animal which he was, until for a moment he shuddered, and died — and that night was devoured by laughing hyenas under a large yellow moon; the moon was watched also by the young couple, for lovers they were.

They stood in the moonlight on the trading post porch.

She kissed the white bandage on his throat.

He stared into the blackness of the jungle and murmured — I wonder if I killed him?

She murmured — I wonder who he was?

She looked up.

The moon was smiling at them.

Real
Magic

THE MAGICIAN ON the stage dropped his glove. Yet he still held a glove in each hand. The elderly performer turned slightly and as if by accident the glove in his left hand fluttered to the floor — yet he still held a glove in each hand. He looks at the gloves as if wondering where to put them down, and then puts them down on the table in full view, but at the next instant two new gloves appear in his hands. He puts these immediately down on the table on top of the first pair and flashes his hands empty so all can see with a gesture that would indicate that he is finished with the gloves, yet at that instant two new gloves appear in his hands. He takes both gloves in his right hand and places them over the back of an empty chair, and lo! there they are — and his right hand is empty, but two new gloves have appeared in his left hand. He takes the gloves into his right hand and flings them into the audience. In his hand outstretched from throwing the gloves, two new gloves appear. He also throws these to the audience, yet a new pair of gloves appears in his hand. He puts the right glove on — and invites a young member of the audience to touch one of his fingers as he spreads the fingers of his right hand wide. The girl touches his little finger. Without taking his other fingers or thumb out of the glove, he takes his little finger out, so that the little finger of the glove hangs limp. He takes a pair of scissors and cuts the little finger off the glove. He now pushes his little finger out of the hole so everyone can see. He then begins picking up all the gloves and as he does so he shows the audience that each glove has only thumb and three fingers, each glove has had the little finger cut off.

35

Members of the audience can be heard to murmer as they examine the gloves which he had thrown out to them for these too have had the little finger cut off, although one person can be heard loudly protesting that when he caught the glove he had examined it, and that it had been whole.

The magician regained the center of the stage, and concluded with these words: "During the First World War I served overseas as many men my age did and I saw a couple of battles. In one of them I was wounded, and at first I thought it was a calamity for I had been left with a deformity which I thought to be grotesque and evident to everyone I met, one which was especially repulsive and tragic for a man of my profession for I was then already a master of card magic, though I'd not yet begun to perform professionally. I then made a discovery which to me to this day seems truly magical — a discovery I shall share with you this evening, and if any of you are ever afflicted by a blemish or a sudden deformity I command you to remember immediately the message of my performance tonight — that message is this: that when you work with people they really don't see your deformities.

"If you could have told me in my twenties that my deformity was going to be invisible I should have scoffed in bitter disbelief, indeed I would have found it incredible that one day I should with a certain pride display — as if I were doing a magic trick — the fact that long ago on a battlefield in France I lost the little finger of my left hand!"

He thrust out his left hand and held it steady so that all could see. What he said was true.

And then as those old showmen could, with his left hand he waved them a gracious, "Good evening!"

The Blazing
Blue Footprint

A FOOTPRINT IN blue ink from a birth certificate was blown up to the size of a football field, and projected in sections one night onto the White Cliffs of Dover by pranksters from Amsterdam, young artists. Ships in the Channel saw it, the bright blue footprint, reported it, and refused to enter the port when they could get no explanation of it on their radios. A squadron of RAF Fighter-planes swarmed around it. Three large naval vessels hovered offshore, and many men studied it through field glasses from the bridge, a blazing blue footprint. Finally landing parties were sent from ships in small boats, battling a choppy sea. Submarines surfaced and turned toward it, torpedoes ready, aimed at — "A blue footprint!" Helicopters swarmed down around it, and at first they didn't see the projectors, which the kids had taken elaborate pains to conceal, and the nearby town panicked — thousands left Dover that night on every available conveyance.

"Before I send you to jail," said the Dover judge to the dozen Dutch youths gathered in front of the bench, "Have you any explanation as to why you caused all this commotion?

"Your Honor," said the youngest looking of them, "I traded my white bicycle for this document because I thought it was a grand thing to have, sort of a collector's item, you know."

He handed the document up to the judge.

"You see the footprint on that paper . . . a bunch of us were sitting around one night, studying it in a sort of admiring

37

way, looking at it through a magnifying glass, and standing off and squinting at it from a distance, and I got the idea — it was *my* idea," he confessed, "I said wouldn't this footprint look wonderful — big as a battleship — flashing luminous on the White Cliffs of Dover. And everyone thought it was a beautiful idea, and so we did it."

"What is this!?" exclaimed the judge.

"It's a real copy of Winston Churchill's birth certificate."

"Do you mean that the cause of all this was Sir Winston's footprint from the day of his birth?" exclaimed the judge.

"Yes, we thought he'd rather like the idea, if he were alive, and that it would make him laugh —"

The judge looked out over his spectacles at the London newsmen rushing out to the telephones.

"I shall have to give this case further consideration," said the judge. "This trial is postponed until after the weekend."

But the trial was postponed again, and later it was moved to London, and postponed again. The youths in London were invited to many parties and were soon in the swim of artistic society, several of them married English girls, some got studios and settled down to work, the youngest one formed a successful musical group — and the trial never did occur, although neither were the charges formally dropped, for to just forget is Justice when crimes are dreams.

Doubletalk French

ONCE UPON A time there was a man who was . . . It's hard to explain.

I don't know what he was.

There is no word for what he was.

He began life ordinarily in the Midwest. When he finished high school he decided he wanted to become a painter, an artist.

Well, he wants to be a painter, his parents ship him off to an art school in New York City. You want to be an artist — you go to an art school — that idea.

When he arrived in New York City he made a discovery. It was 1950, and he discovered something he'd never seen before in his life in the Midwest. What he discovered were the foreign movies — Italian movies, French movies, Japanese movies, and at that time movies were never dubbed, but always had English titles, so that one could actually hear the actors speaking — always in a foreign language, of course.

He became a regular foreign film fan.

He developed a peculiar talent, if such a thing can be called talent.

He learned to imitate the voices he heard in the movies.

He used this talent in two ways:

Par example: when someone would insert a French phrase into a conversation — which he didn't understand, of course — he would say something like, "*Je roi mètre, ânon? Caràrnce nous munnétacit tarqu sé vous. . . .*"

And the person would always look a little embarrassed, and answer, "Well, I only studied French in college three years. . ."

Or they'd look a little anxious, and explain, "I only spent a few months in Paris. . ."

And then he would always tell them that he really didn't speak French, that he was just imitating the sound, that it was just doubletalk, nonsense. . . .

But he'd had his little triumph.

But his grand triumphs — they came at night, when he would walk through the streets daydreaming.

All the characters in his daydreams spoke this doubletalk French.

Sometimes he'd be a great politician, and with great gestures, proclaim, *"Je quoi rein aître!"* . . . well, there's no point in my imitating the other characters in his daydreams. They are easily imaginable. Anyway, these were his grand triumphs.

All art students must study in Paris, and so, when he got into his early twenties he, too, went to Paris.

The trouble began as soon as he got on the boat.

It was a French line. He went into the bar. The bar was empty.

The bartender was polishing glasses, as they do, and the American sat down, and said, *"Je bourait — ah — un pernod!"*

And the bartender said, *"Oui, monsieur,"* and began to pour a drink.

"I'd like a beer, please," said the American.

The bartender frowned and said, "But monsieur, you just ordered a Pernod."

"What!" said the American, "You mean I was actually saying something!" And then the American explained that he really didn't speak French, that it was just doubletalk, nonsense, and that it was just coincidence that he had sounded as if he were actually saying something.

The bartender looked at him a little funnily.

"Well, as long as you have the drink poured, let me try it, *Pernod*, you call this."

He took a sip of the drink, and — Uggggh!

It was sweet.

It tasted awful. He asked for a glass of water, and paid for the drink, and walked out on deck; and as he walked out onto the deck he was thinking that it was rather peculiar his blurting out that doubletalk French, because he really hadn't intended to, when suddenly — he blurted out some more!

He looked around to see whether anyone had heard him.

Someone would think he was crazy just talking to

himself, and particularly if they understood French and knew he was talking nonsense.

Luckily no one heard him.

For as a matter of fact he had been speaking excellent French, and he'd just made a very vulgar, a nasty comment on the morals of one of France's leading ingenues.

When he arrived in Paris he continued to blurt out phrases and whole sentences in perfect French, and this "ability" somehow kept him from learning the language.

He meets a girl. They fall in love.

The girl speaks both French and English, and sometimes she tries to translate these things that he's saying, but they never seem to relate to anything that's actually happening. They're like sentences out of the air, from nowhere.

The girl tries to get him to see a psychiatrist, someone she knows, who speaks both French and English.

The American realizes — well, that obviously there is something a little peculiar happening, but he keeps putting off the visit to the doctor.

One afternoon they're walking along the *Rue Charant-Sant* (that's the theater section of Paris) when the girl suddenly points up at a theater marquee. "Hey!" she says, "Here's my favorite actor playing in a show!"

(Some matinee-idol type; she is one of his fans.)

She says, "I'd like to see this show! You won't understand what's happening because it'll be in French, but maybe sitting in the dark and hearing the voices — maybe it'll calm you down a little."

For the last five minutes the man has been speaking in *both* French and English about how he really should see that psychiatrist. "Maybe tomorrow I'll go."

They buy tickets. The show is just about to begin. They take their seats.

The American stops talking, but she can tell he's tense.

They wait.

And they wait.

And they *wait* . . . and nothing happens.

The whole audience begins to get restless, and they begin stomping their feet, and whistling, shouting for the show.

Finally the American says, "Let's go! Let's go see that doctor. Right now!"

They get up and leave the theater, and just as they are leaving a man comes out from between the curtains and announces that the famous actor has taken ill and won't appear this afternoon anyway, so they haven't missed anything.

They take a taxi to the psychiatrist's office — his office is just his apartment which he uses as his office during the day. There is a pretty secretary dressed in a nurse's uniform, and she tells them, "Please sit down. The doctor's busy right now with a patient but he'll be with you in a few minutes."

The man says, "Aaaah . . . is there a men's room?"

The secretary says, "Well, yes, that door there — but there's someone in there now."

But the man doesn't seem to hear.

He walks over and opens the bathroom door, goes in, and the door closes behind him, and — no one comes out.

The secretary frowns because the other person in the bathroom had also seemed to be in a rather disturbed state. She decides she better get the doctor.

The doctor comes out with raised eyebrows at having his session with his patient interrupted, and goes over and opens the bathroom door.

There sitting on the bathtub is a nude man.

There are two piles of clothing, one on either side of him.

The doctor looks around the bathroom. There's no window. There is no way anyone could have gotten out of the room. The doctor turns to the secretary and demands, "I thought you said there were *two men* in here!"

"But there are!" says the secretary.

The doctor stares at her suspiciously, and then turns to the man, and says, in French, "Well, monsieur, what are you doing sitting on my bathtub with no clothing on? *What is the meaning of this?*"

The man explains, in French, that . . . well, of course . . . he is none other than the famous actor whom the young couple had gone to see that afternoon. "Just before the performance today it got to be too much. I have to talk to somebody about it! For the last several months I've been blurting out sentences in perfect English . . . a language I don't speak! *American* I'm talking! *American*!!! I don't speak American."

And then the man — the same man — begins to speak English.

He explains that he is an art student from the States, and that for the last several months he has been blurting out sentences in perfect French, a language he doesn't speak — "Just like I did just now!" he exclaims. "The things I say don't make sense. They never relate to anything that's actually happening."

Then the man — the same man — begins to speak French again, "You see what I mean when I talk the English!? The things I say never make sense, like voices out of the air, they never relate to anything that's actually happening! And I can't control it! I just blurt the words out! I never know what I'm saying!"

Then the man began to speak English again, "You see what I mean, doctor, like just now when I spoke that French. I can't control it. I just blurt things out. And I haven't the least idea what I just said."

"Well," says the doctor, "Get some clothes on. Come outside . . . and we'll talk about it."

The doctor goes out and speaks to the young girl, who had accompanied the American to the office, and to the actor's manager, who had accompanied *him* to the office.

He returns to the bathroom and finds that the *"man"* is having difficulty getting dressed. There are two piles of clothing on the floor. First he starts to put on one pair of trousers, and then, obviously confused, reaches for the trousers on the other pile.

With the doctor's help he gets dressed.

When he finally comes out he's dressed pretty weirdly.

He has on one blue sock and one red one, one brown shoe and one black one. He's wearing a coat from this pile and trousers from that one.

"Listen!" says the doctor, "This is impossible! This cannot have happened. Two people who were leading separate lives suddenly have only one body. [I mean, Reader, as if your mind and my mind suddenly discovered ourselves in one body — you might like asparagus — *I hate it*.] It is not a medical case. It is simply impossible. This cannot have happened! Look! Why don't we all go downstairs to the cafe and get a *drink*."

While they are following the doctor's advice, as they're winding down the narrow Parisian staircase to the cafe below, I'd like to glance for a moment at the positions of the others:

Par example: there's the actor's manager. You can see he's worried. Here he has a matinee idol, a star — well, I mean a dummy, a puppet, a jerk, someone who would do anything he was told to do . . . for money, for fame, or whatever reason, and through clever handling the manager had managed him into a million-dollar proposition. And the manager senses that from now on the actor isn't going to be as easily handleable as before, if handleable at all.

And there's the poor girl. Here the innocent, naive American art student, whom she loves, has suddenly become her daydream hero, the figure of her most private fantasies, and one can imagine that the actor in actuality isn't at all what she's imagined him to be.

44

Well, they get down to the cafe, they sit down, and a waiter takes their orders, but when he gets to the *"man"* he says, *"Je maitre suare — un pernod!"* And then he adds, "Aaaah . . . gimmee a beer."

"But monsieur," says the waiter, and then he adds uncertainly "Sir . . . *What do you want?"*

"He wants a beer," says the young girl.

"He *ordered* a Pernod," says the actor's manager.

The waiter turns to the man and says, "But monsieur, *you must decide.* What do you want?"

I cannot help noticing that there are two ways this little problem of the drink could be solved. There are in fact two ways in which the grander problems this *"man"* must meet can be resolved. There are, as a matter of fact, two possible endings for this story.

For instance: they can look down the menu and find some drink which they both like. They can compromise. The Frenchman can learn English, and the American can learn French. They can help each other out, learn to tolerate each other's prejudices. They can become friends. Until eventually, though inevitably it must take some time, they can become almost like one person again, and perhaps a more complete person than either of them had been previously.

But there is another way this story could end: They can each be stubborn. They can each insist on having their own way. They can begin to irritate each other, and annoy each other. They can embarrass each other, and play little practical jokes on each other, until eventually they grow to hate each other. And when two people hate each other in this situation — from such hatred — inevitably — Oh! I made a mistake . . . pardon me, my Reader, but I am wrong. I said before that there were two possible endings to this story, but I'm wrong . . . for to any story whatsoever, inevitably . . .

There can be but one conclusion.

The Prime Minister's Grandfather

A WALRUS SWALLOWED a candle, grimaced, made a little face at the taste and decided it was a mackerel, and then dove to the bottom of the Bering Sea, nosing about among cold boulders where the best lobster live. He chose to glide about a foot above a seawood meadow over beside a new Canadian submarine being shown off by the Canadian Secretary of the Navy who was playing host to several members of Parliament and the Prime Minister himself on an inspection tour.

"Mr. Prime Minister," said the captain eagerly, "You asked whether we might see some underwater life and I think this meadow might be a good place."

And he gave crisp orders that powerful lights located on the outside of the submarine be switched on, so that when the periscope was dropped beneath the surface of the water it was possible to view the bed of waving weeds for several hundred yards in any direction, such is the clarity there of those northern waters, such the penetrating power of modern submarine lights.

"This was an expensive ship," mused the head of state, and as if to test its mettle he rapped the wall three times with his cane.

On the other side of the two-inch steel-plate wall was the walrus who was worrying a steel loop that swung loosely on a hinge, used to secure the submarine with cable when the boat was at a dock.

Mimicking the Minister's knock with mammalian fidelity the walrus knocked the steel loop against the ship's hull three times.

"That noise came from outside," said the captain.

The Prime Minister rapped twice against the wall with his cane, and the walrus obviously enjoying the game rapped back — twice.

"Who is out there?" asked the Prime Minister.

"It's odd. I don't see a living thing out there," said the captain turning the periscope this way and that. Fish were often curious about the submarine but today the presence of the walrus had caused them all to flee, and the walrus at the moment was swimming about directly above the periscope, his attention attracted by its turning, but he was out of view.

"May I look," enquired the Prime Minister, and he put his eye to the glass, and at that moment the walrus swam down so that his face filled the field of the periscope's view.

"Good Christ it's my grandfather!" whispered the Prime Minister, aghast and visibly shaken. As a boy of nine he had attended his grandfather's funeral in Toronto, and lately the old man had appeared several times in his dreams, admonishing him to conduct the affairs of state in a proper fashion. *"You protect the wild animals . . ."* his grandfather had said to him in his dream only last night. The old man had wagged his finger at him and in his dream he had felt like a child. *"The walrus, the musk ox, the caribou, the polar bear, the white fox. . . ."* The Prime Minister had awoken in a cold sweat and had clutched his heart with a pang of guilt.

On disembarking from the submarine at the naval base the Prime Minister got on the phone to the Canadian capital, instructing aides and different legislators on his position in regard to the new wildlife protection laws which were to be enacted by Parliament soon.

"Now Mr. Prime Minister," enquired the leader of the Opposition Party whom he had gotten out of bed at an early hour, "the law as it is being written affects the musk ox, the caribou, the polar bear . . . but what about the walrus?"

"What?"

"What about the walrus?" repeated the lawmaker.

The Prime Minister's mind worked furiously. A walrus! Could that have been the face he had seen through the periscope?

"Yes! The walrus!" exclaimed the great man happily. "By all means — include the walrus!"

The Purple Bird

FLUTTERING DOWN OF a purple bird to the plaza near the place where I sat in the sun each afternoon outside my hotel in Yucatan occasioned remarks in Spanish which I could not understand. The bird was as big as a robin, and was purple except for a white spot on its forehead and a baby blue breast. Six wind-worn umbrellas fluttered their tatters over tables in a way that in a cornfield might have frightened off birds, but this purple bird landed on a table one day and the waiter shouted something to his wife in the kitchen. She came outside with three plates in her hands and stared at the bird for a moment and immediately returned to her work, but from inside she shouted out "Mi chinaca tompata que!" And the bird flew away.

On another afternoon the bird landed on the peak of an umbrella and a nine-year-old boy all dressed in white without shoes sang out a song at the sight of the bird:

Chinampala talpo!
Se coro mular . . .
Chinaca tempata!
Me cora mular. . . .

Or at least that's what it sounded like he said to me, but I couldn't understand the words, and his Spanish sounded

48

softly like Chinese as does the Maya language. The boy had oriental eyes, was pure Indian with the classic Maya profile, and he shouted out excitedly in Maya when he saw his parents coming, obviously telling them about the bird, and the bird vanished.

The next day as I sat there I spotted his flash of color up in a nearby palmtree, and I pointed it out to the waiter, saying the Spanish words for "The bird . . .", but the waiter didn't seem to understand me, and he stared a moment at the treetop obviously puzzled. The beautiful bird had hopped behind a frond out of view. After consulting with his wife he returned a few minutes later and waving to me walked over to the tree at which I had pointed and patting its trunk, repeated a Spanish word three times, obviously the name of the tree. I nodded smiling, saying "Thank you . . . thank you . . ." in English. A little later I glanced up at the tree and the bird was still there, moving around among the branches, but I didn't want to engage the waiter in another conversation. I left him a largish tip for he was obviously being friendly, and had tried to help me.

"Simpala te quilá!"

"Orozocar tamin . . ."

"Poche quinar?"

I had half-dozed in the sun at my usual table and these voices mixed themselves with dreams. Only half awake I opened my eyes and beheld the purple bird perched on my knee. Without moving a muscle I was instantly awake. The bird made a small odd sound and flew off to the tree. I stood up and there must have been thirty people standing around me in a wide circle, all staring at me seriously.

I immediately went into the hotel. That evening when I came downstairs there was a flurry of excitement as I entered the small lobby to enquire after mail. Half a dozen people crowded a door that led to the kitchen, all of them staring at me with wonder in their eyes. A small girl tried to smile at me, but she dropped her eyes in embarrassment and stared at the floor. As I walked outside for an evening stroll several customers of the restaurant rose from their table at the sight of me, and gawked.

Wherever I went that night people were friendly. Strangers bought me drinks at the bar.

An old woman selling flowers fastened a perfect beauty in my buttonhole and laughingly refused to allow me to pay for it, chattering away in Spanish saying the Lord knows what.

Continuing my stroll I passed a group of young women outside a church who giggled friendily and also stared at me.

I cut down a side-street as I usually did every evening on my walk, but tonight as I passed people came out on their porches, and several waved a friendly greeting to me, and I waved back, smiling for a moment.

I had become famous in an afternoon.

I left the village the next morning and went into a different state to complete my stay in Mexico, because it's no good being famous when people don't understand.

The Green Gardenia

GREEN GREEN GARDENIA covered with dew, sunlit, planted in a flowerpot, struggling for its existence . . .

Little white marbles had been tossed in the pot to make it prettier.

And the Gardenia thought they were its bones, and shuddered in the breeze, in horror of viewing them, so bare, so bare.

50

If the Gardenia could speak, it would shriek.

But its soul was mute.

In a distant corner of the city, in the corner of a church, an organist's fingers practiced caresses on the ghost teeth of his instrument, and the chords he fingertipped filled the church like a warm liquid, softening its dark red walls like rubber, and the man, more like a squid, breathed the water as if it were the fragrance of our green Gardenia.

The man loved music, and his passion led him to stray churches, like this one, where it was quiet, lost in the suburbs.

In a gray way he was a genius. But the man scratched a livelihood from funerals.

Flames tossed about in the air like oriental angels hula-hulaing on the tips of the white candles, pale, in the colored sunlight shooting through the monstrous windows, through the bodies of some painted saints, a lamb, and a goat.

An eternally tired golden Virgin Mary stared down at him.

She was on the ceiling.

Between two arches she clung to her plaster; as he played, as he was alone, he let his head fall back to stare at her and there seemed to be a glitter around her; through heavy eyelids little violet flashes fell around him from her, through an air of darting swirling dots; and he wondered what the color of her eyes were.

The lamb and the goat became dim, and the hula-hula dancers were demanding more attention, and a cleaning woman came bustling down the aisle talking to herself.

So he stopped, and went down to the corner for a beer, and a bus.

He fingered his coin nervously as he waited on the corner, and was amazed at the loud clang it made as he pushed it in the slot of the automatic fare-taker, and the sounds of the people in the bus rushed over him like a gust of overheated air, making him dizzy for a moment.

He sat down and gave himself to the jiggling of the bus, and stared at his dark reflection on the window, and tried not to listen to a fat woman screaming about something to a skinny woman, who was knitting, and nodding.

He lay awake till dawn. He slept for an hour, and dreamed of a green Gardenia.

"Cantaloupe."

"Cantaloupe?"

He nodded and picked up his napkin.

"Coffee."

"Coffee?"

He stared at the waitress, wondering whether to be annoyed, and he decided she was probably tired too, and occupied himself with thoughts of his dreams, like a child trying to reach his boat with a stick, but the boat was stranded a little too far out in the pond, so he could barely touch, tickle the end of it, and it was very exasperating.

All he remembered was a green Gardenia.

The funeral was at ten.

Somehow he enjoyed his work, the flowers, the weeping women, and the brave men; how many hundreds of funerals had he watched in a little mirror set on the organ, where he watched for signals from his boss? Where were his glasses? Ah! He felt them in his pocket.

The weepers and criers he had classified into gentle amusing types for to take them seriously was impossible, and would make his job, his life impossible — pain was too frequent an experience in the world, he had decided long ago, and laughter was his protection; he wasn't contemptuous of them actually, except when they bored him, as one or two would do occasionally — seeking sympathy, a pseudo-father, or what? Sometimes he couldn't tell, and rarely cared.

The children, though, the confused, sad creatures, he always flirted with, with gentle eyes and tender smiles, to distract them from the sordidness of their relatives and parents — poor children, surrounded by cracking shells, and platitudes, and fear shrinking them in the sweet heavy suds in the metal wash-tub of a funeral parlor.

That green Gardenia!

It kept haunting him, his vision of it, and it kept bobbing and popping into his consciousness as a woman would have, had he been in love.

That green Gardenia!

So soft. Its petals had touched him like the face of a child.

The breakfast clatter in the kitchen, trays and forks and plates, shrill screeching laughter, a businessman belching for a joke, all hit his ears like boxing gloves, and he rushed from the restaurant as fast as he could pay his check.

He walked in the sun.

Past bright, painted wooden houses with iron fences, made of metal tubing, edging the crisp lawns, he strolled, like a well-oiled machine.

Morning!

At the end of the lawned block was a square stone building reaching out toward the sidewalk with an awning and a neon sign.

Mort's Mortuary.

The black hearse always waited like the Egyptian cat, full of patience, for its daily child; on receiving its bundle each day it would purr away as only a Cadillac can; and like a cat it would always reappear each morning, empty and greedy; and what care it got: this sleek aristocratic cat, worshipped like an idol.

He played and did his job as usual; the dead person was a fat man, and the mourners were usual — nothing strange about the early day.

As he walked outside the hearse was pulling away, full of flowers and the fat man — a flower fell into the street from it — it was the green Gardenia of his dream.

He walked into the street and picked it up; it was exactly the same. He touched it to his cheek. It even felt the same.

He carried it home in the palm of his hand. He dropped it in a bowl of water, and sat and watched it on the table.

The Gardenia was dying.

It was dry, and he sprinkled drops of water on it.

He examined it closely with his eyes, and straightened a bent petal.

He blew on it, as if to blow some life to it.

But the Gardenia was dying.

It had been cut, taken from its pot, and sold that morning, and it had ceased to struggle. It no longer wanted to shriek, it no longer felt that terror of the pot, for death had taken half of it already.

All day the man sat there staring at it softly, like a madman, I suppose, staring with soft eyes at the dying thing, and yet it did not die.

Through the night he watched it, and yet it did not die; if anything it seemed to have grown brighter, greener, fuller in the gloom, under the little white light, under his soft gaze, his tender mad affection.

Once near morning he walked away to get a blanket to throw around his shoulders, and when he returned the Gardenia seemed paler, and then to revive again as he blew on it, once more.

The funeral was at ten.

But he did not go this morning.

Still wrapped in the blanket he sat watching the flower, and sun streamed in, and noises came in, and a cleaning woman came in, but he waved her impatiently away and told her to come back later, and still he sat, with big red eyes.

The thing seemed dead.

He picked it from the bowl and held it to his mouth and felt currents fill his head and roam around his body as he inhaled death's perfume and he pressed the blossom to his lips and from these lips came a shriek which brought the

54

neighbors whom he easily convinced that he was sane, and safe.

A Gardenia had spoken, and was dead.

The Cat Who Owned an Apartment

NCE UPON A time a man sat listening to music.

His fingers hung limply over the arm of his chair, his eyes drooped, and his feet rested on a sheepskin-covered ottoman. He breathed shallowly.

An expensive phonograph was twirling in the corner; a booming symphony filled the room, and filled the universe as far as he was concerned, so passionate was his attention. Each note he heard, each quiver of the harp strings, bang of the cymbals, nuance of the violin, snore of the tuba, plink of the piano.

The man loved music. He was a connoisseur.

His Siamese cat sat on the table.

The cat heard the music.

But the cat heard other things too. It heard the honking of automobiles, the sound of the refrigerator, leaves stirring in the wind, a dog barking down the street, someone shout.

The man heard none of this. He was completely absorbed in the music.

Then the cat heard the sound of the window being slowly opened and the floor creaking as a man in a leather jacket, wearing tennis shoes, stepped through.

But the man listening to music heard none of this.

The cat heard the sound of the man's tennis shoes as he

tiptoed across the room, and the sound of a knife being drawn from the leather jacket.

The cat yawned and listened to the sound of the knife as it sank into his master's throat, his master's gasp, and to the sound of the man who was listening to music as he rolled down to the floor — dead.

The cat listened to the murderer as he walked back toward the open window, and heard him climb out onto the fire escape.

Then there was the sound of footsteps in the alleyway three stories below.

The light from the open window shone on the murderer. He jumped off the fire escape onto a wooden ledge which ran along the building.

The cat heard all this. But the cat heard the ledge creak as well. The murderer listened intently to the footsteps.

And the cat heard the ledge creaking and creaking and finally breaking, and heard the scream of the murderer as he fell to his death on the pavement below, and the shriek of the child who'd been passing.

Then the cat heard a funny little scratching noise behind the refrigerator.

A mouse poked his head out, pricked his ears, sniffed, and scampered across the room.

The cat leaped.

He landed on the mouse, and bit.

The mouse was dead. The cat looked around. They were all dead. It was his apartment now.

The
Typewriter
Repairman

A TYPEWRITER REPAIRMAN TRIPPED at the curb, falling forward flat into a puddle on the highway, arms extended, and a truck ran over the tips of his fingers. The truck screeched to a halt a hundred yards ahead, and the driver jumped out of the cab and ran back toward the accident victim now sitting stupidly in a state of shock. His face had gotten smudged with grease and his hair was dripping black oil. Across the highway a State Police car had pulled to a halt, and help was on its way.

*

Fate takes strange turns, indeed — and to think that but a few minutes ago the man was sitting in the author's chair, that writer of short prose pieces whose new book of fantasies *Some Morbid Curiosities* had been reviewed only last week in the Sunday paper. The repairman had read with pleasure the author's two earlier books, and so he felt regret at having been out-to-lunch when the well-known man had brought his typewriter in for cleaning. A glob of honey had gotten among the keys and the typewriter of course had stopped dead, locked in sugar-shock. The typewriter was an old-fashioned upright which typed characters slightly oversize, easy to read, and rather unusual to see these days; it was almost an antique. He'd taken off its ribbon and given it a bath in acid, and when the typewriter was ready and now with a new black ribbon, the owner of the shop decided to deliver the typewriter himself after closing in the evening for he saw to his surprise that the author lived only a few blocks away, though across the highway, where he never had any occasion to go.

The house strangely matched the typewriter being slightly oversize and old-fashioned. It stood alone on the block and was surrounded by vacant lots in which weeds grew shoulder high. It had rained heavily all day, but it had stopped at dusk leaving large pools everywhere, and the fields were full of fireflies. As he entered the yard he noticed a tree on which the fireflies blinked off-and-on in unison like a Christmas tree, and he recalled reading on the dust-jacket that the author's hobby was Oriental botany.

A plain lady opened the door and there were children's voices beyond her. She led him to the writer's workroom on a sunporch and he placed the typewriter on the desk before the author's chair. The first thing he noticed on entering the room was that five humidifiers were silently sending up jets of spray.

She explained that the author would return in a few minutes and would pay the repair bill in cash, and if he would like to wait, why he could sit down right here. He assured her he had plenty of time, that his shop was closed, and that in fact he could do with a rest after lugging the typewriter five blocks in his arms.

"What is that?" he blurted out before she left the room.

He pointed at a very large table that was only a foot off the floor and on which many small plants were growing.

"It's a bonsai mangrove swamp," she explained.

An immense glass box whose walls were only a few inches high contained the shallow waters out of which on small islands the tiny trees grew in profuse entanglement. It was like a regular swamp. Miniature Spanish moss plants hung from the branches. The box emitted a high-pitched humming which he finally figured out was caused by clouds of almost-invisible flying insects that hovered over five finger-length alligators asleep in a heap on one of the islands. The glass box was illuminated from below and light shone through the lakes revealing tiny oysters clinging to the mangrove roots and fish of different sorts, some swimming in schools.

The lady — and the repairman couldn't figure out whether it was the author's wife or not — re-entered the room with a plate.

He said, "I read two of the books that were probably written on that typewriter. I enjoyed them very much."

She smiled. On the plate which she offered him were two clusters of brilliant vermilion grapes, each cluster shaped precisely like a football.

"They're a seedless grape from Burma. He grows them out back."

He bit one of the grapes in half. Its flesh was bright orange.

"He has a green thumb," she explained, and again she left the room . . . which he noticed now as he looked around was rather messy with stacks of books and magazines and manuscripts everywhere. A strong sense of good manners kept him from reading any of the manuscripts, but he began to glance idly at the titles of the books and magazines and it puzzled him to find that they were all scientific works and periodicals, as many on geology and astronomy as on botany. He opened several of the books and saw that they were not popular expositions of their subjects but were illustrated with graphs and filled with Latin words and mathematics, and he found it queer that he didn't see a single work of fiction for he knew the author had never written anything else. The author had been quoted in the Sunday paper as saying, "I never write about real life . . . I only write dreams . . . no one in any of my stories has ever even had a name." But for someone immersed in dreams he showed a remarkable interest in the real world! — said the repairman shrewdly to himself, while searching his pockets for his pipe, and he discovered much to his irritation that he had left it at the shop.

Within arm's reach he noticed there was a hookah on a shelf.

Oho! — he said to himself — What's this?

If he had had his pipe with him it never would have occurred to him to do it, but his craving for his forgotten favorite pipe caused him to put the mouthpiece of the water pipe between his lips, and he inhaled sharply as bubbles sounded from the hookah.

And what is this? — he said to himself as he opened a small circular container that rested on the shelf near the pipe. In it was some blackish-brown sticky stuff.

He said again — Oho! I think I have found the secret of the author's imagination. I'll bet this is opium or hashish or some South American mushroom.

But he replaced the container and the pipe onto the shelf and turned his attention to the typewriter. There on the table was a pile of typing paper and he took a sheet of it and inserted it in the typewriter.

Now on returning a typewriter to a customer it is quite customary for the repairman, before handing it over, to type a sentence on the machine, it being a self-evident demonstration that the typewriter is in good working-order.

As often as not he would type — Now is the time for all good men to come to the aid of their party, but he didn't feel like typing that, no . . . but what should he write *on this typewriter*? This typewriter had never written anything but fancies and dreams, never once the truth. Never once had it written truthfully of the real world, never once . . . but what could he make the author's typewriter write that would be the truth?

As the greatest authors have done, he stared at the blank sheet of paper.

If he hadn't been sitting in the author's chair wanting to write the truth I don't think he would have done it, but without giving it a second thought he said to himself, reaching for the container beside the hookah — I think I'll try some of this.

Using a matchstick he scooped some of the sticky stuff into the bowl of the pipe, lit it, and inhaled deeply, holding his breath to get the full effect.

He stared at the blank sheet of paper. The truth? And college courses in philosophy were desperately recalled from long years ago . . . the *truth*?

He inhaled again a long puff from the pipe.

Suddenly he looked behind him but there was no one. He felt not unlike a schoolboy in an empty classroom about to write a violent anonymous message on the blackboard which would be discovered later by the teacher on entering her room already half-filled with guffawing scholars.

What message should he leave for the author to find? The truth?

He took another puff on the pipe.

The truth is that it was not opium the man was smoking but it was a remedy for plant fungus which had infected the mangrove trees. It was suggested to the author by an old friend who was a florist in Chinatown, and was composed of Japanese snuff and powdered anthracite coal, and given body by a little honey. It was in fact in concocting the stuff that the author had spilled some of the honey onto his typewriter. The author had doubted that the arcana of Chinese herbal medicine included Japanese snuff, but his old Chinese friend had assured him that for many years China had imported Japanese snuff solely for its fungicidal properties. He had been treating his plants several weeks with it and it was proving remarkably successful.

The snuff was harmless enough, and it ignited well, but the anthracite coal powder when it burned produced carbon monoxide, and he had gotten several lungfulls of the poisonous gas and to top it off he had held his breath with the stuff in his lungs furthering its effect on his system. If he had taken ten pipefuls of the poison he would be dead, but luckily he had only four, but it was enough to make him confused, mildly excited, and it caused him to hallucinate. Indeed, even as he types the sentence on the typewriter the poor man is seeing in his mind great expanses of sky and clouds that roll out in a boiling panorama of great distances. Before fleeing the house in exhilarated panic he puts his face close to the paper to read what the typewriter had written, and it is as if it had been written by the infernal skywriter in black smoke,

each letter a mile high, the sentence stretching across the heavens. He had written in capitals on the virgin white sheet:
BORGES IS BETTER

The Weir
of Hermiston

CHARACTERS IN THE follow-
ing story were first drawn by the pen of Robert Louis Stevenson in his long romance "The Weir of Hermiston," which lay unfinished at his death. Sensing that Stevenson desperately wanted the romance to be finished, the raging tensions in its plot to be resolved — I have done so — if too briefly, surely resolutely. The words of my first paragraph were the last words Stevenson ever wrote:

He took the poor girl in his arms, and she nestled to his breast as to a mother's, and clasped him in hands that were strong like vises. He felt her whole body shaken by the throes of distress, and had pity on her beyond speech. Pity, and at the same time a bewildered fear of this explosive engine in his arms, whose works he did not understand, and yet had been tampering with. There arose from before him the curtains of boyhood, and he saw for the first time the ambiguous face of woman as she is. In vain he looked over the interview; he saw not where he had offended. It seemed unprovoked, a wilful convulsion of brute nature. *(R.L.S.)*

"I'll tell the town I saw you two!" shouted a familiar voice from behind a blasted oak. It was Frank Innes.

The startled pair sprang apart.

"Ye canna doot!" pleaded Archie Hermiston timidly.

This Innes now is chinning himself on a branch of the oak, as if to demonstrate his superior muscular strength.

Kirstie, the girl, stands by, hands on her hips, and a black look on her face, grave as a siren can be, she was silent as their graves are now.

She stared from one to the other, and thought of everyone else she knew and how they'd be laughing at her name. She stared first at the weakling Hermiston, and then to the strong man, but never once did she stare to the sky for help, for she was not that kind of a girl to start praying at what she saw to be her own funeral, so to speak.

"Laddies," said she, perhaps to them both, but she spoke as if delivering a judgment for herself to hear, "Ye're nae good! Ye'd be the livin' death o' me! Ye'd make o' ma name a morsel for the fat and skinny to chew. Ye're city boys, fresh as the dresses in the Glasgow shops so smart ye appear to be with your English words, but can ye no hear a country girl's heart when it thumps ye the message and calls your souls by name?"

"Kirstie, be quiet," says young Hermiston.

"Young lady," mocked Frank Innes, "Did ye call ma soul by name? I dinna ken."

The pretty young girl lifted two fistie rocks, and spat viciously on the naked spots where the rocks had lain, and then she replaced the stones, each in the other's place.

She said, "I jest drownit two white worms that nae fishie will iver eat fer his good supper. Did ye ken ma two stringies? Did ye see they was your virrey selves? Lookit!"

And again she lifted the two rocks from their places, held up two "things" (the Lord knows what they were!) in the fast falling twilight for them to see. "The white worms ha' turnit BLACK. These are your virrey souls ye see in ma hands here. LOOKIT!!"

Frank Innes lowered himself to the ground from the branch of the oak tree where he'd been holding on so spryly, but let out a yelp as he landed the wrong way on his foot, twisting it.

Young Hermiston had been holding on to a branch of the same tree, but more for support, as his impotent rage had made him dizzy, and his helplessness in the face of the stronger man's taunts had at one moment nearly caused him to faint; but now his hand tightened around the branch, and with an easy movement, snapped it off the tree, and his eyes gleamed in hatred. He stripped the branch of its twigs to make a clean club. He exulted in an easy strength he knew to be his own, but which he'd never known — until this moment.

While Frank Innes quailed, and felt fear, his stomach quivering like an apple jelly, and he recognized his fright to be his own, that he'd always carried it beneath his belt he'd always pulled so tight, terror that he'd hidden, as if it were his treasure, beneath the bravado.

Hermiston lashed out with the club and broke Frank Innes' left arm.

Kirstie reached under her apron for a knife and rushed it to the trembling right hand of Frank Innes.

"Go it, Laddies!" she whispered hotly.

Frank Innes lunged like a girl with the knife, yet he stuck it straight in Hermiston's stomach, and withdrew it from the flesh in a flash of blood. Hermiston stood there grinning, bleeding, standing over Frank Innes, and says, "Ye think a wee bloody blade can stop a man whose destiny is to kill you?"

Innes backed away into the bushes, his teeth loudly chattering, shrill whimpering his only answer until suddenly he began to emit a staccato of squeals, becoming blood-curdling screams, for he had crawled backwards into a large field of thorns, and Hermiston laughed and followed him into the dark forest of thorns, driving him backwards over the land of a million spikes, and though Hermiston, too, was torn by thorns, he only laughed, and grinned, and chuckled weirdly, wildly.

Through the night they fought until all hours.

Cottagers whose land bordered that forest were woken by their screams, and knew they were ghosts that so ranted through their woods in such wild rage; and they bolted their shutters and cowered inside, a whole family around a candle through the night, even after the shrieks had ceased, until the sigh of dawn, when they began to search the copse, finding many bloody trails that crisscrossed; and finally they found two black corpses, and there was difficulty telling which was which, almost unrecognizable they were, so eaten were they already by white worms.

The
Scotch Story

AN UGLY MAN from Alabama moved to Scotland where his strange accent and foreign ways took the fancy of a high-born beauty of the Highlands, and though he was quite poor and she quite rich, they married.

She would not hear of him working and what was he to do? The judge in Alabama who had sent him to the workhouse had called him a loafer, but that wasn't exactly so, for he'd been making moonshine up in the mountains since the time he was twelve in his own backwoods still.

But he played quite the gentleman in Scotland and with some success, and he was well-liked, and by his many nephews and nieces he was adored; he played croquet well, and he got good at golf; he was a jovial drinker, a jewel of a host, and his wife was a generous soul and their lovely parties were at the heart of the good times that were had in that land.

With a Southern simplicity he was devoted to his wife like a hound dog to a beautiful master.

In the latter part of the Nineteenth Century there was a decade of unusually severe winters and a Great Depression enveloped Europe, and Scotland was devastated by crop failures and business failures, great families fell and many men were broken, and in the Highlands the poverty was appalling, and people stopped playing golf and going to parties.

Several years passed as the misery deepened.

One night the dour Lairds of the county of Glenlivet met in the home of the Alabama boy, grown much older in these few years, yet his wife, though pale and thinner, tubercular (she was doomed to die of it in two years, and her husband with Southern simplicity a week later died of sorrow) his wife retained her glow of beauty through this winter that was polar.

"We must do *something*" said one of those around the table.

"We must *do* something!" said another, his frown deepening and deepening.

"We *must* do something!" exclaimed another, almost weeping.

"*We* must do something!" said another, hopeless.

"Kin ah give ya'll a lil drink," said their host gently, pouring a generous portion into each glass.

They sipped their drinks awhile and sighed, and perhaps it was the liquor, but their sighs grew not so hopeless. Then one got argumentative, and he said angrily, "How can you afford expensive liquor like this in times like these?"

And the man from Alabama explained in his affable and drawling manner that he hadn't bought any liquor in four years, but that it was something he'd cooked up himself.

The men looked at him in disbelief.

They lifted their glasses to their noses, and smiled, and shook their heads in disbelief.

Each took a tiny tasting sip, and rolled the liquor round his mouth, and one laughed and said, "You made *this*?"

Another laughed louder in a more mocking way, and asked, "You *made* this?"

Another chortled almost madly as he doubled-up with

laughter at a thought so outrageous: "*YOU* MADE THIS?" he screamed, rolling on the floor.

"Yes sir, in Alabam' we calls it moonshine."

Where did he make it, they asked. And he explained that he had a little still up aways into the hills, tucked away sort of cozy, where none of them could ever find it. And now it was his turn to chuckle as he thought to himself how he hid it. "You could never find it!" he laughed, as he suddenly imagined them all looking for it.

But how did he make it, they all wanted to know, and he explained that *that* was a mountain secret, and if it was anything he'd learned growing up in Alabama it was *never* to betray to a foreigner the secret of making moonshine. Foreigners being anyone not born and raised in those mountains, and the term included all city-folk, and especially folks from Montgomery, the capital of that state, and where the tax collectors came from. He explained to them: "I promised my grandpappy on the day he died that I'd never teach a foreigner how to make moonshine." He shook his head seriously and said, "And I never will."

"Of course," he said, "it doesn't taste exactly the way it should because I had to make-do with whatever I could get around here, and it's got a strange smoky taste from the peat that I couldn't do anything about, and of course in Alabama we mostly use corn, but they mean something different by corn in Alabama."

But then his eyes lit merrily and he added, "But it's a pretty good taste, hain't it?"

And the men began to point out to him that if only he'd show them how to do it, why they'd start a business, the whole bunch of them there were ready to back him up because in this dreadful winter what the whole world needed was a drink like this, and that if they could start producing it, why people would be driving sleds from London to buy the brew, and each sled would bring a bag of money into the county, and he'd be the savior of them all.

"I could not tell the secret, and break my oath to my grandpappy," he told them.

"In these times, lad," said the oldest and the loudest of the Lairds standing on a chair, "it is the duty of every Scotsman to come to the aid of his country. *Are you not a Scot?*" the old man asked him.

"Me . . . Scotch?" he said thoughtfully, obviously struck by the idea that had never occurred to him before. "But I was born in Alabama," he protested.

"Is this your house we're sitting in?"

"Certainly," he answered.

"And does the land your house is on belong to someone else?"

"Certainly not," he answered, looking over at his wife uneasily.

"This is our land," said his wife to him.

"Well if that's *your* wife, and this is *your* land . . . then you're a Scot!"

"You mean I'm Scotch?" he asked amazed.

"You're Scottish!" they shouted at him. "Are you not one of us?" they asked.

"Well, if I'm Scotch . . . and ya'll are mountain men . . . then . . . then . . . then *you* aren't foreigners!"

They cheered.

"You are my true friends," he said, "and I'll share the Secret with you."

"Perhaps you'll be the savior of the county," grinned his wife. "And I'm very proud to be your wife," she added.

"But what'll we name the new drink? — How about *The Glory of Alabama!*"

"How about *Alabama Moonlight?*" suggested another.

"What about *Alabam' Moonbeam! Alabam' Moonbeam!* That sounds wonderful!"

"No . . . no . . . my friends . . . as I'm the one with the secret, I get to name it . . . my friends I've lived a life in

Scotland that would never have been possible in Alabama, and I would like the name to express my gratitude, and I will be most gratified if it's called . . . simply . . . *Scotch!*"

And so it has been, has it not?

And the Alabama boy need not have feared the anger of the ghost of his grandpappy for that mountain secret has been well-kept in the Highlands.

Orange

THOUGH A MAN may be white from frostbite, purple with rage, yellow from jaundice, green while sea-sick, green with envy, in redfaced apoplexy, turned black by the sea when drowned, or browned by the sun, now gray in horror, or in the pink for pleasure, yet I know of no case that a man may be orange.

Though the villain is black, the coward yellow, and the novice green, I know nothing of the character of that man who is orange.

The human body's fluids, organs, and flesh can be found to be of every hue, except that there is no organ, liquid, muscle nor piece of fat that is pure orange.

Excepting orange, in death we may meet every shade.

There is no word that rhymes with orange.

2

Orange is the best color.

Where this color is present, gloom requires effort.

Good spirits are created in this light.

With fixed, triangular eyes, a jack-o-lantern stares at me, but in vain tries to raise his eyebrows at my thought.

Whatever the candle in the pumpkin sees, it illuminates.

Among great lights he holds his candle, and his grin is not discouraged by the white glare; nor later on the windowsill is he disconsolate at viewing the great dark, outside.

By his light children are transformed into — Good Lord! into what!? . . . (There go a pirate and a rabbit walking hand-in-hand with Death) . . . perhaps, into gods this evening, hallowed, mellowed by orange.

I have asked myself seriously, "Why do the young stare so seriously upon the face of the pumpkin?"

As, even now, I conjure an image of that hideous visage, yet benign, so orange, I wonder — who in history's name could you have been? What life did a body lead to be left so headless?

I have tried to imagine the body of the jack-o'-lantern.

"Are you John the Baptist?"

"No," answers the candle in the pumpkin.

"Are you Marie Antoinette?"

"No."

"Are you that Greek whose body the women tore apart, whose head they left in a cave, where it alone survived and prophesied, and then allegedly was lost — are you that head, priest of poetry and music, Orpheus, himself? Is this what you've come to?"

The pumpkin is silent.

Perhaps he is embarrassed because of his teeth, or contemplates the Bittersweet.

The Hunger
of the Magicians

A STONE LAMP at an altar was lit by a flaming wand.

It was two thousand five hundred years ago to this very moment, in Greece.

It was a hot gray morning.

Overhead stormclouds are streaming by, but for months there's been no rain. Soon they will hear distant thunder, but still there'll be no rain, and very soon thirst and famine will finish them.

Out of saintly stubbornness they will starve to death, for they would not leave this place, this stronghold on Mount Olympus.

But now look! The lamp illuminates the lighter's face.

He wears a pointed hat.

Perceive the hat: it is two heads high, a cone, precisely wrapped by a single piece superbly cut — of gray stuff — heavy and rough, a giant swatch of undyed wool which falls from his cone to his toes, leaving a place for his face and hands to be free, forming a complete cloak.

It is the dress of a magician.

The master has a gray beard.

In his hands the light burns brightly. Look! There are fifty-two gray beards. The room is full of pointed hats. Their heads are bowed. All hats point to the lamp. It is a den of magicians!

In unison the masters groan in monotone the various vowels.

They wear no garment between their skin and their grotesque gray hats. Between their skin and their bones there is no flesh.

Here are the greatest magicians in the world, this is the Golden Age of Greece, these are the men behind that scene — but drought and famine have hit the countryside. The thrashing streams of Mount Olympus are dried up.

Nobody brought them any water or food.

And it made them mad.

Indeed, it was less than five minutes ago that the lighter of the lamp, the Young One, spoke up with a sublime assurance to his elders. This is what he said to them five minutes ago:

"The world is not going to forget this.

"I place the memory of this outrage inside the altar lamp.

"The sight of our miserable state shall rest here in the lamp until five hundred years has passed five times, until that veritable moment — and then — it shall flutter free of the lamp and enter the head of a writer whom it'll madden for an evening, for he shall see us all here, and write it, and perpetuate this scene in the Literature of his language; and whatever language he writes, all the shining Literature of that language shall be transformed at that instant into lamps of rock more durable than this stone lamp, for that tongue shall survive to become the only language spoken on earth; at the moment when the vision flies, fifty-two writers of that chosen language shall become aware of the *hunger of the magicians*; they shall come as close to death as we are now; they shall witness vanity in horror and forget themselves; then Greek gods will be reborn; in them our light shall shine again; they shall refashion that language: new letters shall be added to its alphabet, and, as pigeon, it shall flutter between Hebrew and Chinese, and crystals of grammar in silver syntax shall be worked with ornaments from ancient tongues to transform it — they will make that language ready to write the history of the world; in their dreams they'll see what has duration in a language, and each in writing shall see a secret of perpetuity.

72

"I plunge my wand into the water, and . . . ah! I have speared a fish!

"Let us eat! Let us savor this moment of time.

"I plunge my wand into the fire. How quickly it catches!

"I destroy my wand to do this deed. This vision of us is our property, our land forever, and to sign the deed we must light the lamp.

"Magicians, great scholars, seers, if . . . it is your will?

"How brightly the tip of my wand flames.

"They shall see us everywhere, our quiet stare, in every line they write — a haughty mien, our silver smile of mercurial weight.

"For noon has come, and doubt is gone. There are no shadows anywhere.

"Now at last remorse surrounds the sources of our memory like purple light, the Godhead is bowed in blight . . . all our thoughtful frowns are snaked, our dragons are drowned, our lions are suffocated, our eagles are grounded. . . .

"And if, when tomorrow comes with bells, Sorrow slaves at many works — then jonquils will be carried by canaries to this bright yellow spot, and sports will be performed by plants running on their roots . . . like a merry-go-round the great oak spins . . . and when, to a trembling touch, stone faces bend . . . petal-thin flesh shadows we can lift from the ground . . . blue jay's flash of sound. . . .

"The sound of the seer is heard like a blue jay's shriek in the inner ear as it cuts crude consciousness away.

"Those fifty-two writers shall witness vanity in horror and forget themselves."

The stone lamp at the altar is lit.

The Institute for the Foul Ball

H E HIT A single, stole two bases and then stole home, winning the game which had gone into the eleventh inning, and it won a minor league pennant for his team.

The three had seen enough! Three men had come to Louisville solely to view the young player in action. One was chief scout for the Detroit Tigers, the second was the venerable and long-time owner of that club, and between them sat the Tiger manager. While the fans in the stands went wild at the fantastic conclusion of the game, those three men sat quietly and smiled at one another, for they owned his contract.

His nickname was *The Cheetah*. They called him that because of his amazing ability to run fast like that big cat, to spurt off at high speed, stop, and reverse the direction of his running, and each reversal of direction served to increase his speed. This, of course, is just the talent one needs to steal bases, and during the Cheetah's first year with the Tigers he broke the world record for stolen bases before the season was four-fifths over. But it was not merely speed, for he seemed to have the sixth sense of the hunting cat, he seemed to sense in advance the intentions of his opponents.

To watch him steal bases was a beautiful sight.

Nobody ever fooled him, and he was the trickster *par excellence*.

He was not a powerful hitter. Perhaps the oddest record he held was that of being the only regular major league player never to hit a home run.

74

He was a place hitter. And he could be relied upon to hit an infield grounder, or to bunt, but with unerring instinct he was able to hit the ball to just the place that threw the whole infield off balance. He invented "the soft hit," that is, when he'd hit the ball it would slowly lob anywhere from five to fifty feet and fall to the grass without bouncing, and the place it landed more often than not was an exactly equal distance away from each of three or four players, so that each made a dash for the ball and frequently fell over one another trying to field his puny hits. Spectators and sportswriters soon noticed the frequency of those queer collisions, and the cruel crowd found it funny to see grown men crash into each other, saw it as comedy and cause for high hilarity, and greeted each new "accident" with gales of laughter. You can imagine how it made the players feel.

The infield got paranoid. They got overcautious about running for a ball that another player was also after, to such an extent that it became not uncommon that players who ran after a ball he'd hit would all suddenly pull up short and freeze to avoid colliding with one another, and none would dare or deign to reach down to pick up the ball, each of them standing staring at it like a crystal ball-gazer in a trance — and during this the runner would have gotten safely to base on a hit that any one of them might have turned into an easy out with a throw to first.

He was also the inventor of the "in-place, spinning bunt." This curious method of hitting a ball could only be used when the pitcher threw a low fast ball. Holding the bat as if to bunt, he would suddenly turn the bat vertical, and sharply waggle the bat as it met the ball, and a loud *crack* could be heard, the bat would shoot straight up twenty feet into the air, but the ball would shoot straight down to the ground, landing an inch or two in front of home plate, and it didn't bounce away, but stayed there spinning like a top with such a velocity that if the catcher tried to grab it with his bare hand the ball invariably leaped forcibly out of his hand as if it had a life of its own.

His great skill with the bat was acquired through much practice. No other player ever worked as hard practicing place hitting, and every day at dawn he practiced for several hours on the empty field, assisted by a catcher, sometimes several young pitchers, and a couple of kids whose job it was to chase the balls and to move the target.

For he had a cloth archery bull's-eye which lay flat like a flag on the infield grass, and he would have one of the boys move it into whatever position he was trying to hit the ball, and it was the boy's job to stand near the target and note where the ball came to rest. The brilliantly colored circles of the bull's-eye are marked with numbers, and armed with pad and pencil, it was the boy's job to keep score. Thus in a systematic way he labored at dawn day by day to achieve his ambition: to hit *any* ball that a pitcher might throw — to *any* precise location on the infield.

"To hit any ball that a pitcher might throw—" seems like a straightforward phrase, its meaning quite clear; yet it meant something quite different to him than it might mean to you or me, or than it meant to any other professional player. When a batter stands in the batter's box waiting to hit the ball there is an imaginary rectangle over home plate. If the pitcher throws a ball which goes inside this rectangle the batter is obliged to hit it, and if he does not the umpire calls "Strike!" However, a batter is not obliged to hit a ball that goes outside this rectangle. Well, he felt obliged.

He felt it was the duty of a batter to be able to hit any ball that his bat could reach, and much of his practice was devoted to hitting balls that others considered "Inside," "Outside," "High," or "Low."

He attained his ambition, and he always struck at every ball that was thrown by the pitcher.

He taught himself to hit either right- or left-handed, and while other batters tried to hit the ball squarely, his method was to hit the ball off-center, and he mastered the art of giving the ball just the right amount of spin so that when the ball first touched the ground it stayed there, rather than bouncing farther across the field as might be expected in the direction he hit the ball. And it must be noted no infielder ever got used to his hard-hit grounders that miraculously stopped abruptly when they first touched ground, and often a foolish mitt could be seen clawing the empty air at that place where by the laws of physics the blasted ball should have been.

But the most bizarre hit he ever invented (called "the laser" or "the mirror hit") was rarely seen, for it could only be used when the pitcher threw a fastball directly at his head. He would point the bat like a rifle at the pitcher, and then with all his strength he would shoot the bat forward to meet the ball as if he were making a billiard shot, hitting it head-on with the tip of his bat; but there was no controlling the direction of the ball, for it could only return on the exact path it had traveled; but such was the power he put into the bat that it returned at twice the speed like a bullet toward the pitcher.

He had some funny "ideas" about baseball.

1. He believed that a batter should be allowed only one strike.

2. He believed that the concept of four-balls-and-you-walk should be abandoned.

3. He believed that there should be only one batter's box, and that it should be located directly over home plate.

But let me explain more fully about these three ideas on how ideally baseball should be played, or, as he said, how it *shall* be played in the future. He believed that the batter should stand on home plate squarely facing the pitcher. If the pitcher threw the ball to his left the batter would hit it as a left-hander, but if the ball were thrown on his right side, well, then the batter would hit it like a right-hander; and if the pitcher threw the ball straight toward home plate, why, he said, there were a number of different ways to hit it. Instead of the imaginary rectangle he saw an imaginary semicircle very much larger that was determined by the reach of the hitter's bat. That is, the batter would be obliged to hit any ball that his bat could reach. If the batter failed to swing he was out, or if he swung and missed he was out. One strike and you're out. But if, by chance, the pitcher threw a wild pitch, a ball that went outside that semicircle, that the batter couldn't reach, then the pitcher would be automatically taken out of the game, and the batter would get another chance to hit.

The owner of the Tigers was a good guy. He had acquired considerable wealth through canniness, and in the process had acquired wisdom, and from the first he took a liking to the young athlete, invited the youngster into his home, and often the young man joined his family at their rather elaborate and formal dinners where he became a favorite of the old man's wife. On the very first of many, many such evenings, after dinner, the young man had been explaining these ideas he had about baseball, and the old man asked, "What happens if the batter hits a foul ball?"

"He gets another chance to hit," answered the Cheetah. And then he added, "But the foul ball is the key to the Mystery of baseball. There should be an Institute for the Foul Ball where scholars and scientists would bring all their intelligence and scientific equipment to bear in studying it. For there is something about the foul ball, I feel it in my bones, that will prove to be the key to the future of baseball."

And the old man said, "I own a factory, and on the grounds of the factory there is a whole building devoted to research, and sometimes there are ten or twenty people working on a particular project or problem that we think important — is that the sort of thing you mean? Do you mean that I should hire ten people to study *the foul ball?*"

"No," said the young man. "It would have to be a much larger effort. It would take hundreds of people, a real institute, with everybody studying, and it would be staffed by our best ballplayers as well as scientists."

78

"You mean all these people would do nothing but study *the foul ball?*"

"Not *only* that," the Cheetah mused. "They would also study the Home Run Pitch."

"What the devil is that?"

"Well, it should be possible for a pitcher to throw a ball so that when it was hit the ball would go two or three times as far as might be expected. In other words, a ball that you would expect, when it was hit, to just go over the second baseman's head and not much farther, would in fact sail right over the center field fence for a home run."

"What!?" exclaimed the owner of the Tigers, and it must be admitted that this gentleman spilled his glass of sherry onto his white summer suit at this juncture, and began to sputter almost angrily out of pure astonishment. "What possible reason would any pitcher have for learning that pitch? Can you imagine any possible situation in which it could be used? Why would any pitcher ever want to throw such a ball?"

The young man sheepishly said, "You know, I've given considerable thought to that, and it's rather odd, because I haven't been able to think of a single occasion in which a pitcher could use it to advantage in a game. And yet, you know, it's *possible*, and I think at the Institute they would choose to study that possibility."

The old man sighed and scratched his head. "Son," he said, "I'd like to get something straight about you — do you take this seriously? This idea of an institute where there would be hundreds of highly trained people studying the foul ball, you do see that such a thing could never be, don't you? If I read about it in a story, perhaps I'd be amused, or I can accept it as a beautiful daydream of a young ballplayer, but it can only exist as a fantasy. You do see that it is not really possible?"

The young man sensed the earnestness of the owner's

question, and he answered levelly, "If the people love baseball enough, and if they want *their* team to win badly enough . . . they will create such an institute. I must add that I think it more than just *possible*, I believe it probable, in fact, inevitable, and *soon*."

"In your lifetime?" asked the sixty-year-old man.

The young man smiled gently, and answered respectfully, "Sir . . . in your lifetime."

"My boy, do you have any conception of what it costs to have even twenty highly trained scientists work on a problem? Well, let me tell you it costs a fortune."

"Couldn't you get money from the government? I mean, baseball is America's national sport."

"That is unrealistic. I frankly find it difficult to believe that you could be so naive. I believe that you think I should sponsor this project, and I wish to make it clear to you that I won't."

"Really? Gee, I hoped you would because I can see it would take a person who could organize things, and of course, it would take a lot of money. I thought you'd be just the person for it. It would make you famous . . . I mean, your name would go down in history as one of the most important people in baseball. You'd like that, wouldn't you? In the history books you'd be as famous as *me!*" And the boy flashed a brilliant smile expressing his genuine affection for the older man, who was studying him with great perplexity.

But the boy's smile faded, and his brow clouded, and he said desperately, "But you *must* start the institute. It will be dangerous for you not to . . . Couldn't you sell your factories? Aren't you sick of being rich?"

"Dangerous for me? Now what does that mean?" enquired the rich man, laughing icily, while pouring himself a Scotch over a spherical ice cube.

"For goodness' sake!" exclaimed the Cheetah. "The danger lies in that someone else will get the idea and make it reality. Suppose, instead of us, the Indians start the institute!"

"My boy, I'm well-acquainted with the owner of the Cleveland Indians, and I want to assure you that neither he, nor any other owner in America, would do anything but laugh outright at the notion that they pay millions of dollars to support an institute to study the foul ball and (God forbid!) the Home Run Pitch! Besides, the way you say that baseball will be played in the future — I can't help noticing that those new rules just fit your style of hitting. You, and only you, would do well. I think those rules were tailor-made to give yourself the advantage."

"That is not true! Let me tell you how my ideas about baseball came about. When I was fifteen in the orphanage at Louisville . . ."

"You are an orphan?" exclaimed the owner's wife who had been listening attentively.

"I was found by the cook in the snow on the front steps of the orphanage when I was only a few days old. She called me her little Eskimo and said I looked like a Laplander baby. She said the only mark on my body was a spot on the end of my spine which disappeared, she said, three weeks after she found me. I've always thought that my parents must have been American Indian. But all that's not important! Let me tell you how my ideas about baseball came about . . . I remember it so vividly . . . I was sitting in a classroom at the orphanage, and my English teacher was reading aloud to the class a book called *Moby Dick.* . . ."

"*Moby Dick!*" exclaimed the lady.

The boy paused, puzzled, mildly pained at her interruptions, but deferentially he turned to her and explained, "Moby Dick was the captain of the ship in the storybook . . . but all that isn't important."

"But it is extremely important!" snapped the lady. "You're all mixed up."

"As I was saying," smiled the young man, "I wasn't listening to the story, my mind was having its own thoughts, and I was thinking about *baseball*, and I noted how often even

in big league games the batters hit balls which were caught —
flies and line drives and foul balls. I figured maybe a third of
the outs in every game were caused by such hits. And I figured
if those outs could be transformed into singles, why it would
be of tremendous advantage to a team. If the batters could
guarantee that their hits touched ground before they were
caught, then . . . then . . . no one would ever hit a home run! I
suddenly saw a flaw of baseball: greed for home runs causes a
ridiculous number of needless outs. I stared at the moving lips
of my teacher, but I didn't hear a word. I immediately saw
that stealing bases would assume a new importance among
batters who only would single, and at that moment I knew I
should become a great runner. I saw my future clearly then,
what now is every day. On that very afternoon I signed up for
track, but of course I never learned to run, I learned to stop,
and, in stopping, to swing in an inner circle that sends my
body flying off in the opposite direction. I discovered how to
do it within a month of that afternoon, and within three
months I figured out the three rules for future baseball. The
thing I didn't realize that afternoon was that once a batter
takes his eye off the outfield fence, and instead, only aims at
the infield, then he gains in control what he lost in power, and
the possibilities become vast for variety, so to do the
unpredictable becomes easy. It's easy to hit balls that are
"High" or "Low" or "Inside" or "Outside," if you're only
aiming for the infield. It's easy to bat and run the way I do,
and anyone could learn it, if anyone would take the trouble to
try. The present-day rules concerning "three strikes" and
"four balls" are from a different era when everyone seemed to
have more time, and I'll bet, when the players weren't so good.
The truth is that the times have changed, and baseball is
becoming old-fashioned. The game is too slow. Baseball is
boring."

"But, it's what I've always said," laughed the lady.

"You have always been *ahead* of your time, my dear,"
murmured her husband.

But the Cheetah ignored their banter, and continued seriously, "We love the fans who love baseball, but sir, have you ever considered the people who don't like baseball? Don't you sometimes wonder why? I've been thinking about them. I think a lot of those people are going to become baseball fans when my new rules are adopted, for though home runs will be rare, there'll be lots of action, and the game will go at a faster pace, and there will be *a new drama* in every play. Don't you see? The pitcher is obliged to throw a ball that the batter can hit, and whatever ball the pitcher decides on, the hitter is obliged to swing; and except for the case of a foul ball, everything will hang on a single pitch, and each time the pitcher winds up, each spectator will be on the edge of his chair. Statistically it will be evident, and to everyone it will be quite clear that there is more to be gained in trying for a single than in trying for a home run. But there will be occasions that can arise in a game — for instance, in the ninth inning when the other team has a two-run lead, and there are two men on base, a man might come to bat, and perhaps, if he felt a certain faith in himself that man might throw good sense, logic and statistics to the winds, and the man might clobber the ball, and it's possible that that man might hit a home run. It is difficult for us to imagine now, so sated at seeing several home runs in a game, what those future fans will feel who witness that event, or how the great crowd will respond, yet I think it safe to say that the home run then will be seen in its true light, and as something more marvelous, befitting of baseball, more like a miracle."

The Tiger owner's wife said, "If baseball were religion, I think you'd be a saint."

2

The forthright lady turned and to her husband said, "Well, what do you think?"

"Very interesting," he said — yet he will find this evening unforgettable, will find occasion to recall with rue the ring of truth in the words of the Cheetah, but far more memorable in his mind is what comes next, for the evening is not over — and indirectly, what comes next, by his own estimation, will make him the happiest man in the world.

The slender beauty whose hair is pure white, who is all things to him, is first and last his wife; she'd been a sort of super-secretary while intimately sharing his earnest reflections; she had had a hand in all his deals, each scheme had had her touch, and she was his perfect partner in those strange plots, necessary, no doubt, to a self-made man in becoming a magnate in the world of heavy industry; and their faith in themselves has never flickered for an instant in forty years. It is especially poignant that the marriage of so perfect a pair could be marred by something anybody else would consider unimportant, merely that she didn't like baseball, yet so it was. It is his sad obsession, and has been his lifelong daydream, that she should sit beside him in his box to watch the Tigers play. But alas, instead, she had conventional interests not unusual for a wealthy woman — she was a trustee at the Art Museum, and she supported the Symphony; yet literature mostly occupied her mind — she was a real reader, and she had read everything. To a timid suggestion by him that she might join him in watching the Tigers play, she invariably would reply, "I'd rather read a book!"

This lively, lovely lady then touched the young man's arm, and said, "Will you come into the library with me. There is something there I would like to show you."

The old couple lived in a mansion, and the young man followed the lady down a marble hall and into a deeply carpeted, great dark room that was illuminated by a single reading lamp, where books were everywhere, scattered all about. She explained, "If I ever let anyone clean up in here I'd never be able to find anything." She took a book from a shelf and opened it to the first page. She waved him to a chair, and she herself sat down, and she said to him, "Call me Ishmael!"

84

"What is that?" he asked.

"It's *Moby Dick*!" she replied. "I'd like to read some of it to you, if I may."

He nodded assent.

"Only this time," she laughed, "I would like you to *listen*."

He said he would, and indeed, he did, his eyelids drooped and he sat quite still; as phrase conjoined to phrase, sentence after sentence, and paragraph piled upon paragraph, as her eye skipped suddenly from the bottom of a page to the top of an adjoining page, and later as the page was turned, or the chapter ending reached, during that impalpable pause when the periods on the page turn bright green, her voice took off its clothes; by that I mean those rags of her personality in her voice (by which one might recognize her on the telephone) were somehow dropped away, and revealed the genius of the English language quite nude; and a naked anonymous beauty danced from phrase to phrase. I think it was the muse. And as she read you might have said at certain moments that Herman Melville himself was in that room, that it was *his* voice, readily recognizable by the Nineteenth Century idiosyncrasies of his speech, but that momentary phantom from another time is but another costume of a voice that vanishes in a rush of sparkling grammar, and the voice of the work itself revealed itself. They heard the voice of Moby Dick, those two. That night they heard the song of the great white whale.

As she read, she forgot she was reading, and as he listened, he forgot he was listening, so enrapt did they become in the tale, and chapter followed chapter and the minutes passed majestically.

Why does it seem unusual that a young baseball player should deeply experience a work of literature? Well, that is what happened.

The minutes passed by quite differently down the hall

where the owner nursed a Scotch, and after a while he began to wonder what had become of the two, and wandered down the hall in search of them. Quietly he approached the library door which had been left ajar, and he stared inside, surveyed the dark scene, saw the two, saw their profiles and had the sense not to interrupt.

He returned to the sideboard to replace his glass, reached for the phone, called the plant, and had a long chuckling conversation with a labor leader; he glanced at his watch and saw that it was five o'clock in Italy and he called his representative in Rome; then he spoke with Washington, and he talked with our Senator there, and several others; he called San Francisco to wish a grandson happy birthday; then he rang the garage, and gave instructions for the morning to his chauffeur.

Now he raised his eyebrows at his wristwatch, and returned to the library determined to interrupt them, but the lonely echoing of his footsteps in the darkness damped that determination, and his steps were still as he approached the door, and for several minutes he listened to the sound of her voice, not making out the words, merely listening to the distant dance of syllables; and he wondered whether her throat weren't getting tired.

With new determination to be patient he quietly retreated, got himself another drink, and sat down in a comfortable chair, closed his eyes, and his recurring daydream re-occurred: it was a sunny day at the ballpark, the fans were on their feet cheering, and his wife was beside him, laughing and obviously enjoying the game. That was all there usually was to the daydream, but now it began to go differently than it ever had before, for the man fell asleep in his chair and the Forces of Night began to play in that idyllic ballpark: a cloud crossed the face of the sun. The stadium was cast in shadow. Low storm clouds raced across the sky. Lightning struck the flagpole, and the flag went up in flames. An explosion on the pitcher's mound created a crater rapidly filling with water. The baseball fans began to riot. Violence was in the air. Shrieking bodies began falling from the upper decks, and his wife says to him, "This is why I don't like baseball!"

Luckily this likable man never remembers his dreams, and now he fell into a deep and dreamless sleep and for twenty minutes he hardly moved a muscle.

He awoke to the sound of the grandfather clock, and was himself in a moment, and to himself he spoke. He said, "It seems incredible that they could still be reading that book. It seems incredible," he said aloud in the empty room. "But is it possible that my outlandish plot is working?"

Several days ago when the Tigers were playing out-of-town he'd been watching the game on television and his wife had happened by and for a moment her eye had been attracted by a close-up picture of the Cheetah on the screen, who was about to bat. "What an interesting face! Is he Oriental?" she had exclaimed.

"He is American. He's from Kentucky," he'd answered. "I don't know what his ancestors were."

And she had watched the Cheetah hit the ball in one of his weird ways, so that it stopped abruptly between the pitcher and first baseman, both of whom ran for the ball. The pitcher got it, and snapped the ball toward first base where he thought he saw the first baseman, but the ball hit the umpire on the nose. Next she watched him steal two bases, and she watched the infield commit two ridiculous errors which were really hard to believe, and the crowd began laughing, soon falling over themselves laughing, unable to stop, and she witnessed forty thousand baseball fans possessed by the devil of infectious giggling.

She had smiled.

He had seen it from the corner of his eye.

Although she had continued on her way, and had not inquired as to the outcome of the game, still it was a start, it was the first pleasure she had ever taken in watching baseball.

The old man figured that perhaps if he could get his wife to take a personal interest in a player, then it might follow as a matter of course that she would become interested in the game, and it was with this idea that he had invited the Cheetah to dinner.

Now his footfalls echoed happily in the darkness of the hall, and as he approached the door ajar, he called his wife's name, and opened the library door, found the wall switch which illuminated the great globe of a chandelier, and flooded the room with light.

The old man beamed at the blinking pair, unable to hide his delight in their friendship, and said, "I think you got carried away."

The Reader and the Listener arose, and she closed the book.

Quietly, he said to her, "Don't lose the place!"

She stared frankly and deeply into the young man's eyes, and quietly answered, "I won't forget!"

Yet stubbornly the youngster stood there staring at her with an urgent question, the mute appeal eloquent upon his face, and for a moment she was bewildered by its meaning. And then suddenly she saw it, and she said, "Tomorrow!"

"After the game!" he whispered.

She turned to her husband and asked, "If you are driving home after the game tomorrow, can you bring the Cheetah with you? We have an appointment."

"Certainly!" he said.

She left them, and the old man saw the Cheetah to the door, and offered to call a cab, but the Cheetah noted that there was a full moon perfect as a baseball, and that he would prefer to walk awhile . . . for what after all is more wonderful than walking through the sleeping suburbs with the lines of a great book rampaging inside the skull, when one first is beginning to grasp the idea of destiny and that the stars are right.

Back in their bedroom the owner said, "The Cheetah is not an ordinary player, and it would not surprise me if he becomes a real star, I mean a favorite of the fans, for already they are beginning to applaud when he comes to bat. Yet he's just a kid from Kentucky, and he doesn't know anything. Fame can throw him off balance. Soon he's going to be adored, and there'll be a million people after him, and he's got to learn how to handle them. He's got to learn to meet all kinds of people. I would like you to invite the Cheetah to our dinner party for the Prince of Persia next week — and if you would, I'd like you to take him under your wing, make sure he's dressed properly and knows which fork to use . . . in a word, I want you to *educate* him, if you would, to the world."

"You mean . . . I should be *his teacher!*" she exclaimed in utter astonishment, and she added, "I think you have been reading my mind!"

"I have *not* been reading your mind!" he snapped irritably, "You know I never know what you're thinking."

"That is true," she said. "Well, let me share my thoughts with you. Tonight something very beautiful happened while I was reading to the Cheetah. You know, I have read *Moby Dick* several times, and I have in the library everything Melville ever wrote, but tonight I experienced that writing in a way I never did before. I witnessed something inanimate come to life, and I feel just as if I'd witnessed a miracle. I'm sure the Cheetah saw it too! I'm going to read out loud to him every book in the library!"

"You can't be serious," said her husband. "Let's get some sleep."

And so the light in their bedroom was turned out, and soon the man began to snore, but wait! the snoring ceases, and his wife who was lying there wide awake, thinking that he might have woken, half-rose out of bed to look at him and was startled by an uncanny smile upon her husband's face. In fact, the man was dreaming.

He dreamed he saw the Cheetah juggling seven baseballs.

That was all there was to the dream, but it went on for some time, and the man obviously was delighted by the performance; but it is really of no consequence, for this man never remembers his dreams.

The lady got out of bed and donned a robe and put on slippers and made her way through the great house to the kitchen to prepare a cup of tea, but all the while she tried to figure out what had happened in the library. With steaming cup she made her way through dark rooms of silence until she reached the place itself, and found the book. And she read a few lines out loud but it was no good, for there was no magic. For the magic to occur, it was obvious to her that it was essential to have a listener; but not just any listener, it must be someone who really listened, like the Cheetah, for she sensed that his eyelids quivered at each nuance, he had angelic sensitivity, and she had heard him take a sudden breath at a turn of the tale, a moment before Ishmael first saw the white whale. But why was it important? Perhaps because she was such a reader, and she sensed that it would happen with every book she read to him, all the familiar books, which she knew, might come alive, be quite different, be quite new. She saw clearly that in all her reading she had missed something essential, that it takes two people to read a book, a Reader and a Listener, that only then can the voice of the work itself come to life. But what was her relationship to the Cheetah? It surely wasn't sexual, and the woman had three grown sons, and she recognized nothing in her feeling for him that was maternal. Could it really be so, what her husband suggested, was she to be his teacher?

Her husband suddenly appeared in bare feet at the doorway, and she answered with silence his serious stare. "What are you thinking of so late at night?" her husband asked.

"The Cheetah," she said. He made to return to his bed,

90

but she called out to him, "Wait! What is it? What can it mean? *The Baltimore Chop. . . .*"

And he explained that that was a baseball expression which she perhaps heard used by someone speaking of the Cheetah, for, as he said, "It is one of the Chectah's favorite methods of hitting the ball. Like a lumberjack with an ax, the Cheetah raises the bat above his head and brings it down with all his might, smashing the ball straight down into the ground in front of home plate so that it bounces high, high into the air like an infield pop-up fly. It doesn't matter if someone catches the ball because it's already bounced once. The ball has to be thrown to first in order to get the runner out, and frequently a good runner like the Cheetah can get to first base ahead of the throw. That's a Baltimore Chop. Let's get some sleep."

"Wait!" I have many more questions to ask. If I show up at your office tomorrow at one, will you take me to lunch? And afterwards, I want you to take me to . . . I want to see it myself, the game!"

3

In five years' time the whole world would know that the Cheetah was a champion, but during his first season in the major leagues only his running was regarded remarkable, and at that, he was considered a clown.

There is an odd group of men who always dress in white, who devotedly make the trek to the ballpark each day the Tigers are in town, but who never see a game. They are those concessionaires of Coke and hot dogs and beer who work behind long counters built along the inner corridors of the stadium; and there are certain old men among them who have held that same job year after year, who have sharp ears, and who have become connoisseurs of "the roar of the crowd," and can make remarkably good guesses at what is happening on the field by merely listening to the booing and applause, or the spirit in the roar when the fans suddenly stand to cheer a play.

But this year these old men began to hear a sound from the crowd which they had never heard in the ballpark before — it was laughter, it was everybody laughing out of sheer delight at the Cheetah, for to watch him steal a base was like watching an impossible magic trick performed before your eyes; for when the Cheetah hit a single, and the next man came up to bat, why the pitcher, the first baseman, the second baseman and every fan knew that very probably within the next few minutes the Cheetah would try to steal second base. Each spectator was expectant, and a hush would fall as everyone waited for him to break, and the tension became terrific, and there! doing exactly what everyone was waiting for, right before their eyes, the Cheetah would steal second base, and the infield would blunder, and the crowd would break into uncontrollable laughter. And often, even when he failed and was tagged out, as sometimes happened, as he walked off the field toward the dugout the crowd would rapturously applaud him for having made a good try at doing what delighted them, for as I said, the crowd considered him a clown. One reason no one took him seriously was his batting average, which at first was nothing special. His hitting was erratic, and though he had developed the rudiments of his style before he reached the major leagues, it was during his five years with the Tigers that he perfected it. Slowly but persistently his batting got better each year, and consistently he got better at doing all his tricks. During his first two years with Detroit the sportswriters, especially those from out-of-town, were wont to refer to him as the "Kentucky Kid," often in a rather patronizing way; but during his third year this nickname was used less frequently, and then it was forgotten, as people in the baseball business to a man stopped laughing, and everyone began to realize the Cheetah was a champion.

The statistics tell the story. Here are his batting averages for those famous five years:

In 1979 he batted 238.

In 1980 — 288.

In 1981 — 338.

In 1982 — 388.

And in 1983 he batted 438, the average improving precisely 50 points each year.

Now a knowledgeable person with a nose for statistics can tell there is something slightly astonishing about these figures.

For one thing it can be seen that in his fifth year he sublimely *tied* the all-time hitting record made by Hugh Duffy in 1894; but furthermore those figures show a *constancy* well-nigh incredible, reflecting surely his *perseverance* practicing place hitting at a time when others would consider themselves lucky to be sleeping.

Sublimity, constancy and *perseverance* are, no doubt, the attributes of many superior men, but there is more than that to being a champion — one must win, and moreover, one must win at the right time.

But only the champion can lose at the right time. Only the champion can — at the right time — choose to lose.

Let me show you what I mean.

In the Cheetah's last year with the Tigers (it was the Tigers' last game of the season) and there were two outs in the top of the eighth when the Cheetah came to bat for the last time. The Tigers were ahead 10-2, and unless the visitors scored eight runs, this would be the last time the home team would be at bat.

It had been the Tigers' greatest season, they'd won so many games they'd clinched the division championship a week before, while the visitors were in Last Place, so this final contest of the regular playing season was not what you'd call an important game, except in one respect. The Cheetah was coming close to breaking the all-time record for a season's batting average, and the stadium in Detroit was jammed, filled with fans who wanted to see him do it. To heighten the drama of it the ballclub had altered the scoreboard, adding two new boxes, one of which showed the Cheetah's average, as it changed hit by hit, and the other showed the number of hits he needed to break the record. He'd hit well that day, bringing the average up to a point so that now he needed only one more hit to break the record, while if he struck out, he'd merely tie it.

This record is the most venerable in baseball. Most records in sports over the last hundred years have been rather regularly broken. Generally in each generation somebody breaks the record. But the record for a season's batting average was made in 1894 and has never been surpassed. Now baseball fans are devoted studiers of statistics, and there is not a living fan that can claim to remember any other name at that spot in the roster of all-time records, any name other than *Hugh Duffy*. That name, his record, intrude like a bright beacon through the darkness of time from that legendary land of oldtime baseball, lend it relevance, and create continuity between the days of yesteryear and the game we play today.

The early part of the eighth inning passed as in a dream. The spectators weren't paying any attention to the game, and everybody began talking to one another excitedly, and the sum of all these conversations was a steady roaring drone so loud that you couldn't understand what the person next to you was saying, so that everybody had to talk a little louder in order to be heard.

As the Cheetah stepped into the batter's box, the noise from the excited crowd if anything grew louder. Here was a crowd, if ever there was one, that was ready to cheer the victory of a champion.

The pitcher stepped on the rubber, about to pitch the fatal ball, when suddenly the Cheetah stepped out of the batter's box, calling time out for a minute. He stood there with the bat in his left hand and that hand rested on his hip, while with his right hand he took off his helmet and scratched his head with it, and looked up at the sky, for all the world like a man who was trying to figure something out that he didn't understand.

Finally he turned and spoke to the umpire who was standing behind the catcher, and staring seriously into the old man's eyes, he asked, "Should I break the record?"

This man was the senior umpire in the American League, and had devoted 30 years to studying the fine points of the rules of baseball, and perhaps more than any other man in the world was equipped to answer any question concerning any situation that might arise in a game, so that it was really quite appropriate that the Cheetah should ask him his opinion.

The umpire could not say yes or no.

Instead, he removed his black hat, and scratched the top of his head with his finger while he pondered, and Lord knows all that went through his head as he weighed the matter.

Finally the old umpire answered, "When somebody breaks Hugh Duffy's record I think I'll retire. It will mark the end of an era, and I am part of that era that knew that long-dead Duffy had been a better batter than any living player could ever hope to be. When that ancient record is taken off the book, it'll be a new ballgame, and I, I am part of the old ballgame."

"Listen! Tell me this!" exclaimed the Cheetah to the umpire urgently, "What'll happen if I fail? I'll have merely tied the record, so they'll let Duffy's name stand as it always has, only below or beside it, they'll put my name. To have my name beside Hugh Duffy's . . . what greater honor could there be? Am I right in what I say?" he demanded of the umpire.

The umpire answered, "That is the way the record would appear."

The Cheetah said to the catcher, "You signal the pitcher to throw three balls straight across the plate. I'm not going to swing. I'm going to let the umpire call me out."

"I understand," said the catcher.

And so the Cheetah stepped into the batter's box, and the catcher signalled. The pitcher threw the ball over home plate.

"Strike!" called the umpire, thrusting his right hand into the air.

Suddenly there was silence in the ballpark.

The catcher threw the ball back to the pitcher, and all the pitcher had to do was lift his mitt in order to catch it, but the pitcher failed to do this, so the ball sailed past him, and had to be retrieved by the second baseman, who walked over and handed the ball to the pitcher, who was plain flabbergasted, as was every fan in the park, at the Cheetah's failure to swing, because for five years it had been the Cheetah's style to swing at *every* ball thrown by the pitcher, and no umpire had ever had occasion to call a ball or a strike when the Cheetah was at bat, and now for the first time in five years he had failed to swing.

When the pitcher threw the second ball he was so nervous that the ball went out of control and came across the plate so low that the catcher hardly managed to hold on to it, but again the umpire's right hand shot out, and he shouted, "Strike two!"

The Cheetah half turned his head and muttered out of the corner of his mouth to the umpire, "Thanks!"

And the umpire muttered so that only the catcher could hear, "Better get that pitcher in line!"

The catcher flashed the pitcher the sign, and repeated it vigorously for emphasis, and the pitcher nodded, and threw a ball that sailed right through the very center of the imaginary rectangle, and such was the silence that each person in the ballpark heard the umpire shout, "Strike three! You're out!"

There followed a long moment of stillness in the ballpark during which it would probably be correct to say that the only movement in the stadium was that of the Cheetah walking back to the dugout dragging his bat along the ground. There was no wind and the pennants and flags hung limp upon their poles.

But a sudden breeze set the flags to fluttering, and the moment was over, and the players on the field began to move. The Cheetah's out had retired the side, and now it was the visiting team's last turn to bat, and as they left the field, the Tigers came out.

The spectators all understood that the Cheetah had failed, but that he had failed they could not understand. They were dumbfounded and the fans began quickly to leave the stadium. Their exit was orderly and the whole crowd left as fast as they could, and as they quietly fled they looked at one another quizzically, and shoulders were shrugged, and all were chagrined.

Meanwhile one of the weirdest half-innings ever played by two major league teams ensued. Though it was of course theoretically possible that the team at bat might rally and score eight runs to tie the Tigers, and send the game into extra innings, nobody for a moment believed such a thing might actually happen. Everyone knew, every player on both teams knew, that the Tigers would win, and that furthermore, no one cared whether the Tigers won or not.

As the ninth inning began the last of the spectators disappeared, leaving the stadium empty except for those whose business kept them there. The players looked around in wonderment as the first man came up to bat. The pitcher threw a ball, and then a call-strike, then another ball and then another call-strike, then another ball and then finally, at last, another call-strike. As if under the spell of the Cheetah's performance, the batter hadn't swung, but had allowed himself to be called out on strikes. But the pitcher seemed to be taking an inordinate amount of time at it, and everyone was itching to get off the field. The next batter again took the full count, and when the sixth pitch was thrown, he hit a line drive into left field and speedily ran to first base. The coach at first base said sarcastically to the player, "What are you trying to do, start a rally?" The player blushed. There is one thing that can make a baseball player blush. It is the sarcasm of a coach. The runner felt like a fool, for he realized all of the players wanted nothing but to end the inning as fast as possible, and to get off the field. His getting a hit was an utter waste, and was merely time-consuming.

The next batter came up, and again the pitcher threw three balls, and two call-strikes, and when the sixth pitch was thrown the batter did not swing, but the umpire startled everyone by calling, "Ball!" The catcher stamped his feet in irritation, as the batter walked to first, and the man on first moved over to second.

It would probably be correct to say that at this point everyone in the ballpark felt as if he were about to lose his mind. Would the game *never* end?

The Tiger manager was so angry that he replaced the pitcher, but this only served to make the inning last a little longer.

The runner on second had his special agony: he was ashamed that he'd been so idiotic as to hit a single, and in his nightmare of embarrassment, desperately he asked himself — What would the Cheetah do in my position?

Suddenly he broke into a run, as if trying to steal third base, and the pitcher threw the ball to third and the man was tagged out. The runner on first got the idea, and he too broke into a run, trying to steal second base. And he even made a good show of it, sliding into the bag, but he also was easily tagged out, ending the game.

The happy Tigers fled the field and found the locker room filled with writers. Indeed, it was as if The Baseball Writers' Association of America were holding its annual convention in the Tigers' locker room, for every prominent baseball columnist in the country had come to Detroit for this game, to witness the Cheetah break the record, and now it was the duty of each to find out for his readers what the devil had happened. Each player found a photographer standing on top of his locker, and three television networks had live cameras centered on the catcher who had come into the Tiger locker room to recount for the whole world the conversation he had heard at home plate between the Cheetah and the umpire. And the umpire, standing nearby, immediately corroborated what he said. The Cheetah amazingly managed to get into the shower for these few minutes, eluding the cameras, and when he emerged, draped in a towel, and the microphones and cameras turned to him, the drops of water on his body caught the television lamps, and on the television screen he was seen to sparkle as he spoke, and he was the perfect picture of a champion. His face expressed pure pride, and he did not have the manner of a man who had failed. He said, "The proudest day of my life was when I broke the record for stolen bases back in 1979, and each year since I have broken my own record, and each year it makes me feel proud."

He stood aloof, apart, his gaze directed a little to the side, and down, as he spoke with grace of pride — but suddenly his whole demeanor changed, he seemed to shrink a half an inch, and he became before their eyes an ordinary troubled human being, and looking directly into the cameras he spoke from his heart, and the sentiment he expressed touched the heart of every baseball fan.

He said, "I would not have been proud to have been the one to take Hugh Duffy's name off the roster of all-time records."

And suddenly everybody understood — that the Cheetah cherished the ancient records, those Nineteenth Century statistics, and that they themselves did.

Had the Cheetah broken the record many men would have blinked and dimly known that yet another wrinkle in their brain had been smoothed out, but when he chose to lose, it made them stop and think, and they found that they were moved; for baseball engages the heart in a manner no other sport can, nor Art.

In a work of art "sentimentality" is rightly regarded as an unforgivable sin, and that there must be no sentimentality in a work of literature is quite true; however, I must say, it puts any author of a baseball story in a peculiar pickle, and I should like in passing to point out that in real life men only do good deeds, never vicious things, from sentimental motives.

It was said that everyone understood why the Cheetah had chosen to lose, but there was one fellow who couldn't, an Englishman who's a film critic for one of our national magazines, and it was his opinion that the Cheetah decided not to break the record because the fans had booed him in the first inning when he had sacrificed instead of making a hit.

Now generalizations about groups of people are more-often-than-not incorrect, and are merely exaggerations of intangible things; however, such a statement will be made, and it is quite correct, true — and furthermore might be instructive for a foreigner who would understand our game.

This is the statement: *Baseball fans are more sentimental than other people.*

Than, say, hockey fans, or basketball fans, or cricket fans.

Baseball fans have "a sense of history" no Englishman can hope to comprehend who was raised playing cricket. The critic's English education left him well-equipped to understand American movies, but not the Cheetah's motives when he chose to lose.

If one could get copies of all the statistics that have ever been compiled in the history of the world, and set them all up alongside one another so that it would be possible to fairly choose among them, and one asked the question: Which set of statistics is held to be *most sacred?*

The curious question has only one answer: *The Official Baseball Records.*

The European sports of soccer and cricket have no comparable body of statistics.

I mean — *Why do they say Babe Ruth is immortal?*

Why, indeed. A thousand years from now every religion practiced today will have utterly withered away, present-day governments will all be gone, no existing university will exist then, but baseball will survive through all the changes of those thousand years, and The Official Baseball Records during all that time will be kept assiduously; and Duffy's name will be there and the Cheetah's name below it, followed by a hundred other names of hallowed hitters who had followed the Cheetah's example, had tied the record, but not broken it — a most illustrious list; and as the oldest institution on earth baseball will have its historians, some of whom will specialize on The Twentieth Century, and one of those fellows, pondering the people of our time, might well in wonder ask: Why during the first century of baseball did they say Babe Ruth was immortal?

Why, indeed. But there is no answer to that question, for it is a part of the True Mystery of baseball.

A famous sportscaster, known by his family and associates to be the most callous and cynical of men, actually wept on his national television show while explaining to his listeners what the Cheetah had done.

And baseball fans all over the world that night — perhaps to the extent that each at one time or another had doted on and studied those statistics — felt a gush of gratitude for the Cheetah, and a strange esteem.

And even young children understood that in losing the Cheetah had done a generous and noble thing. And as every child knows, nobleness is the attribute of the champion.

4

"Is it lonely being a champion?" asked the Tiger owner's wife.

The orphan sighed deeply.

"I have hardly had time to be lonely," he answered. "And yet, there have been times . . . you know, I practice hitting every day at dawn, but frequently I arrive an hour early at the field while it is still dark. The nightwatchman lets me in, I change into my uniform and sometimes when I walk out onto the field the stars and moon are blazing overhead; but at other times it is overcast, it is pitch black out there, but I can make my way down the third base line to home plate, carrying a couple of bats. Perhaps I feel around on the ground and find a few pebbles, and I stand at home plate, throw a pebble into the air, and I practice hitting in the dark. Sometimes I pause, and I wonder what it's all about . . . baseball. I look around and wonder what I'm doing there, standing at home plate in the middle of the night. And I realize that I am the only person on earth trying to hit every ball that can be thrown; and that I alone know how important the ability will be for the future of baseball. Especially on such nights I see that I am utterly alone, but then . . . then . . . it is at such times that I most vividly see *him*."

"Whom?" the forthright lady asked.

"The Abominable baseball player," the Cheetah said, squinting as if trying to make out a figure in the far distance that was in his mind.

"Who the devil is that?" laughed the owner.

"It's a kind of joking name I gave to a real person, an actual individual, a man who must have lived five million years ago."

The lady said, "But the ancestors of Man five million years ago cannot properly be called 'men.' They were probably more like chimpanzees."

"Exactly!" said the Cheetah. "I once saw a movie about wild African animals and it showed a roving band of male chimpanzees encounter a leopard. Several chimpanzees grabbed long sticks and waved them like clubs, threateningly, and others began to throw things at the big cat, stones, bits of wood, anything that came to hand.

"At the time on earth that I imagine, the ancestors of Man could do no more.

"They knew no more than how to wield a club and throw a stone.

"Yet more and more they were becoming what we might call men. For instance, when one found a good club, he'd hold on to it, carry it around with him. It was his club. And he learned to do more than just wave it in the air, he learned to *hit*. Eventually he learned how to hit hard, to grasp the club with *both hands*, swing it back, and bring it forward putting his whole weight behind it, so that he could knock out a leopard with a single blow.

"And when one would find a good stone for throwing, one more-or-less spherical, one that fit well in his hand, maybe about the size of a baseball, why he'd hold on to it, carry it around, and after throwing it he'd go and find it, and he could recognize it at a glance. How many million years did it take to learn to throw a stone? They got good. One could hit a bird in flight.

"But a beast can wield a club and throw a stone. A chimpanzee can do as much, if not so well.

"This is the scene I see five million years ago.

"Imagine the beasts, our ancestors. A roving band of nine or ten males emerge from the deep forest onto the edge of a clearing. Some carry clubs. Some carry throwing stones.

"There sitting in the sun in the center of the field is *another* band of nine or ten males, who also have clubs and stones, who shout, and leap to their feet at the sight of visitors.

"At other meetings they might be friendly and curious, but here — they're furious, for the field is the heart of home territory, and over behind bushes are several females dawdling with their babies. The largest of the males, obviously it is the head beast, steps out in front of the others and shakes his club angrily at the intruders, who continue to advance until the two groups are separated by a distance of about sixty feet, whereupon the leader of the intruders (the visiting team, you might say) pitched his throwing stone, a fastball aimed at the foremost of the furious beasts.

"The beast at whom the stone was thrown, utterly without reason, not knowing what he was doing, without a notion as to what might be the outcome of a thoughtless action, stepping lightly aside, he grasped his club with both hands, swung it back, and putting his whole weight behind it, swung the club forward hitting that stone head-on, as if it were the head of a leopard, smashing a hard line drive that went a little to the right of the pitcher perhaps, hitting a companion in the stomach, knocking the wind out of him, so that both the beast and the round rock fell to the ground side by side.

"The one who'd pitched the stone looks down at the rock which had fallen beside his friend, and he sees *it is his own stone*, the one he'd just thrown! And he excitedly points it out to the others. It would seem like a miracle to them!

"And the crack of the bat when the club struck the stone — what could they have thought it was? No one had ever heard anything like it before. The club swinger would be a magician to them. Would they throw down their weapons and flee? Or would they throw themselves down at his feet? It hardly matters.

"But later on that afternoon the one who'd hit the stone would get to wondering how he'd done it. Probably he'd get a friend who had a couple of good throwing stones, and somehow he'd say, 'Get over there and pitch a stone at me, I'd like to try something . . .' And so would begin the *Abominable batting practice.* And it would take a lot of practice but the fellow could get good. And most important, *it was the kind of thing that he could teach to his son*, for it would perhaps be another two million years before they would discover flint and begin to fashion tools which were sharp, so for two million years the trick with the club and stone would be considered miraculous, and those who could do it would be considered magicians."

"Wait a minute!" said the woman. "That *Abominable batting practice*! The way that prehistoric man would stand there — his stance: he would try to hit the stone whether it were thrown on his right side or his left side, whether it were high or low — that's the way you say baseball will be played in the future!"

"Yes, I think the fans will recognize that stance immediately as being more natural," admitted the Cheetah. "But you know, although they practiced for a million years those primitive hitters could never do more than try to hit the stone as hard as they could, and yet, you can bet — each one would *wish* he could control the direction of his hits, but because of the irregular shapes of the stones it would never be possible.

"In mastering place-hitting I am fulfilling the daydreams of two million years of magicians. Knowing their wishes are with me — how can I be lonely?"

The Cheetah smiled at the lady.

The owner said, "That the most primitive man might have hit a stone with a club does not seem to me to be unlikely or unusual, and I think to call it a miracle is exaggeration."

"Don't you see?" said the Cheetah, "A beast can wield a club and throw a stone, but . . . *chimpanzees do not have magicians*. Only human beings have magicians. At the crack of that bat those beasts became men. That was the miracle. The most ancient chord in the memory of man is the thrill that's felt by a baseball fan at the crack of the bat.

"It was the First Miracle.

"And was he not, indeed, a true magician?"

PLEASURES
OF THE IMAGINATION

64 Beginnings

There are different kinds of writing. For instance, there's the kind of writing where you walk over to the typewriter, sit down, and write a first line. You go into the kitchen for a glass of water, light a cigaret, all the while thinking of what you've written. You return to the typewriter and write a second line, then you write a third line, and oh — all sorts of things happen, and there — you find you've written the last line, and if what you've written is any good, then it's all of a piece, as if the whole thing were implicit in the beginning.

As if you put your hand in the water and catch a fish by the tail.

However, there is a different kind of writing: you sit down at the typewriter, just as before, and write a beginning. But when it comes to writing more — nothing happens. You have many thoughts, your mind is aswim with phrases, but your hands don't move toward the keys. Finally, you begin again, and write a new first line.

I have a big old wire wastebasket which I never empty in which I put things that I think I might work more on, and over a number of years it's got chock-full of beginnings, false starts *some might say, failures perhaps — but I've made a book of them, or what-you-might-call a book, of sixty-four examples of this nameless genre of writing. And I have given them names, just as if they were regular stories.*

Sometimes I wonder whether there are real stories implicit in such first lines — you might say virtual *stories, not unreal, but existing in some never-never realm not inaccessible perhaps to certain readers who do themselves indulge in the pleasures of the imagination. . . .*

109

In London

In London yesterday a lorry lunged, sideswiped a fog light and plunged into the Thames. The plainclothesman who surreptitiously was following me broke cover, took a whistle from beneath his cloak and blasted the alarm, rushing to the embankment, abandoning me in the yellow fog.

The Miserable Ostrich

Walking down a desert road in a sandstorm a six-foot ostrich with a painful broken toe staggered with the wind behind him, wagged his wings wildly each time his left foot touched the sand, until finally, for the first time in his life — indeed, for the first time in ten million years — the ostrich flew like an ordinary bird, rose two hundred feet into the air, soared for five minutes here and there. . . .

CROAK!

The red berries of Fall — each scarlet ball rebounds the colors of the call of the scarlet tanager. Green frog— CROAK!—the water lily on which he sits trembles, and a careful eye could see green rings radiate around it, startling a dozing dragonfly.

An iridescent insect walks by.

Gong

It's hard to hold a hammer with your arm in a sling while carrying a gong during the rush-hour on the subway in Tokyo.

The Floodwaters

The floodwaters left a ring on the outside of the bathtub.

The Daymoon

A racing fog enveloped the ship for a number of minutes, a stinging mysterious mixture of mist and hail making haloes of rainbows around the golden white lights of the ship.

It is the boat of my dream! But this cold railing is no dream. . .

Last night while sleeping I dreamed that I looked across a bay, or perhaps it was a wide river, and I saw a large yacht, a streamlined boat with perhaps eight portholes along its side, and in my hands I held a miniature replica of the same boat. It was about a foot long. Somebody said, "It's the *Daymoon*."

The Opera Singer's Vacation

On her vacations the famous opera singer lived alone in a cottage on a small island where she practiced to her heart's delight, and she could be heard at all hours like a faraway bird by wild animals on the most distant shores of the Canadian lake which lay at the bottom of an uninhabited valley.

The silence at the center of a becalmed lake is for her the most beautiful sound in the world.

The Arsonist at the Zoo

The poisonous orange salamander of Peru in its glass cage at the Staten Island zoo attracted the gaze of the arsonist (wearing blue sneakers and carrying a rope in his belt) who had broken in at midnight to start a fire, but had become distracted from his insane design by the liveliness of the nocturnal animals; not that they were wild or especially noisy — they were merely awake and alert. The great cats were playing with their cubs, the raccoons were chasing each other, the primates played quiet games, and the place was alive with moving reptiles. After an hour he left without having started a

fire and he never returned to that scene of what could have
been his greatest crime.

And he never set another fire, but he became a drunk,
closing the bars each night and staggering home at dawn.

There is something about us, we who are nocturnal, that
nobody can ever understand.

The Elk

The elk that fell through the ice reared up on its hind legs
in the shallow stream, falling over on its back upon the ice. It
rose majestically to its 7-foot height and tip-toed away.

Coat of Arms

Once upon a time there was a coat of arms . . . an
extraordinary garment constructed by a tailor-lady out of old
coats customers had left at her shop and never called for —
the coat had twelve arms, altogether, gathered in a circle at
the top, so that when worn, five limp sleeves hung down in
front like elephant trunks, and five hung down in back like a
crazy cape.

The coat had no opening in front, it was slipped on like a
sweater, and indeed it had no front, for the wearer could turn
it whichever way he pleased, this time choosing the velvet
sleeves, or the next time perhaps thrusting his arms into the
tweed, or the black plaid.

The Flabbergasted Reader

The flabbergasted reader closed the book but held it in
his hands, turning the book this way and that, studying the
edges of the pages almost as if he were reading the title on the
binding, all the while musing, pursing his lips, shifting his
weight from one foot to the other, full of thoughts, he touched
his forehead, and outside, the summer-evening silence began

112

to shimmer with the sweetly insistent sound of giant raindrops.

The Tornado of Snow

The brilliant white funnel of the tornado of snow dances atop an iceberg, vividly undulating against a sky that is black and yellow and brown, while below in the bay a blue whale suddenly surfaces beneath a giant waterspout. The boat is bobbing so, I can hardly write . . . I think it's my turn to row.

The Orchid Grower

The orchid grower looked like his plants. Strange purples and browns blotched his complexion on livid wattles, flesh suspended like ear lobes from his forehead and cheeks, sprinkled with light white moles. He lived in his greenhouse, a rather large complex of buildings, a veritable labyrinth of glass roofs and walls where for years he had conducted a successful business in tulips and dahlias — but his pride was his orchids.

The Celestial Sirens

Riding, being carried, lifted by a high wind a thousand feet in the air, 10,000 katydids silently swarm on the wings of a great ascending glider, and suddenly, as the silent ship enters the white heart of a cumulus cloud, 10,000 katydids, as one, burst into their joyous song resounding as sirens here where shadows swim in fog.

Cape Cod

Atop a sand dune at Cape Cod a girl in a red and brown dress waves a yellow scarf. A crow and a seagull for a moment hover over her. Thunderclouds boil above them — they part, the seagull and the crow, and the clouds, and the sands are flooded with sunlight. At the foot of the dune stands a young Indian chief, and he raises his longbow in a graceful greeting. Taking great jumps she rushes down the dune into his arms. At that very moment, on that very August afternoon, Lao Tzu was born, but there it was midnight, and there was a New Moon.

Dishes
The obese puppeteer washed the dishes in the dark.

The Sacred Cow
The sacred cow stumbled in the mud, blinded by tropical rain, lurched forward onto the ooze, twisting its neck awry as it fell; and one of its long curved horns slipped between the roots of a tree, like a key in a lock, so that when it lumbered to its feet its horn was held fast and its snout pressed down into the mud; for five minutes it struggled and the next morning was found, a great white beast drowned in a puddle.

The Sunken Subway
On Thanksgiving Day the subway sank and the holiday riders stood in water up to their chests and then — single file — they all managed to escape up a ladder through a manhole that let them out at Herald Square into the midst of the Holiday Parade.

The Fans of Van Gogh
I saw all the fans of Van Gogh, all past and future ones, all the millions fluttering about in the air, making the sky

black in back of him, all trying to get a peek over his shoulder as he sits there, very hungry, and looking not unlike a scarecrow in the sunshine in the middle of a wheatfield, painting the crows.

I Thought You Were Writing
"I was afraid to say anything to you because I thought you were writing." It was his muse who spoke.

What Happens Next?
None of us could get out of the way.

There was nothing we could do.

Those ten seconds when we saw it coming toward us seemed an endless time.

There was no transition, no pain. Suddenly we were no longer there. We were here . . . listening to your story. But I don't mean to interrupt . . . you were telling us a story . . . what happens next?

The Ghost Town
About two hundred houses roasted in wreck under a Western sun.

Only wild cactus grew in the gardens.

The fence boards fell off and lay in their places, the gables were gray, and whole houses were weathering away. Not a speck of paint was visible.

Dust reigned.

Things with thorns flew through the hot air, and balls of tumbleweed raced through the empty streets.

Cucumbers

Cucumbers by the billion bombarded Paris, dropped from the skies by angry French peasants; they had hired a horde of Piper Cubs to fight a price-war with their government; the cucumbers fell down chimneys, fell into children's sandpiles, landed on lovers in the park, hit thieves while at their second-story work, covered the lawn of the British embassy, pommelled tennis players, dropped into the poorhouse. . . .

A Very Ancient Dwarf

He parted his beard in the middle, and tied the ends to his two big toes, but this only a very ancient dwarf can do.

An Imaginary Biography

"I should like to write a short biography of Poe pointing out that the heart-breaking miseries of his life were a hoax perpetrated by his publishers, and that he actually led a happily proper life, wintering in Samoa, playing in amateur theatricals in Paris, with a cook from Peking to placate his Epicurean appetite, he was a collector of objects made of mother-of-pearl, and danced too much, his wife said, with her maids when he returned home from his famous binges with young Baudelaire."

The Listening Reader

The old-fashioned key was as big as a pistol and weighed three-and-a-half pounds.

His bedroom was circular and it had no door.

The man had a dagger tattooed on his nose, and he slipped into bed without any clothes, donning earphones and spectacles, he adjusted his ashtray, got his book in hand and twirled the dial to "distress" on his short-wave radio, while

116

beginning to read.

It is the lighthouse keeper of St. Lisle.

The Stamp Collectors

The brown stamp on the envelope was carefully removed by a jet of steam from a teakettle by the eight-year-old collector in Venezuela who had just received the letter from Pennsylvania, from an older collector who lived in a tiny house in the woods, who had been snowbound for three weeks, who had been a sailor since his youth and had become familiar with the oceans, for forty years the lookout in the crows'-nest of a clipper ship, come home old to his birthplace to die in comfort, whiling away the time, doting on his stamp book, cared for by two orphan girls; and with a fine Spencerian hand he kept up a constant correspondence with those living in many foreign lands — for he had a wife in Borneo, Alaska, Australia, Norway, India, Malta, and in China, as well as Venezuela.

All his grandchildren collected stamps.

What About *That*?

What about that? A broken arm, a black eye, amnesia . . . found raving drunk in a cheap dive with your pockets full of diamonds.

Attic Animals

Walking up the narrow stairs, dark and dirty, to the brightly illuminated attic, afternoon sun ablaze through three windows, I saw a mole running in circles in a square of sunshine on the attic floor.

I had a feeling there was someone else in the room. I whirled around, and there sitting in a chair which had been

117

covered with a sheet sat Beelzebub, my friend's cat, staring at the mole.

The attic was filled with the sound of buzzing flies.

The Saloon
Where doppelgangers meet . . . that's the kind of saloon it was;

Four Snow Leopards
Four snow leopards in transit by train to the Cincinnati zoo were by accident loosed from their cage, and unbeknownst to their sleeping keeper, they leaped from the slowly moving boxcar at sunset, together disappearing into a Kansas field burgeoning with wheat that stretched as far as the eye could see. It was not until midnight when the train pulled into the Chicago station that their absence was discovered.

A small forest rose like an island in the sea of wheat. The leopards made for the trees. In a month there will be snow.

My Dentist Story
"The book that glitters with mischief
The writing most sparkling with glee
The pages that jump at my touch —
Your teeth — that is the book for me!". . . sang the mad dentist, dancing a jig on a tilted dental chair, shooting novocain into the air; he made a leap for the ether and smashed it, to which all the dentists and nurses and attendants at the Northern Dispensary Clinic who had rushed to the scene, succumbed. He stood on the dental chair and stared in wonder and triumph at the dozen unconscious forms around him. As his co-workers slept their deep sleep, before he left

them forever, to vanish into the labyrinth of the non-dental world, there to become a respectable old sculptor — he pulled all their teeth.

A Jumpy One
The evening was a jumpy one, the mosquitoes were insufferable, the distant drums were wild, their pet monkey spit in the soup, and so it was no wonder, what with the piano out-of-tune, their servant in tears, her best dress torn by a thorn, that the wife of the escaped convict was fed-up.

The Fish and the Hermit
The verandah overlooked a canyon, the canyon held a thrashing stream, and in the stream there was a luminous fish, visible from above on dark nights, for which in his loneliness the hermit fished with a net on the end of a long, strong string.

The only shining object in the dilapidated shack was a large empty fishtank filled with water and illuminated by a deep-purple bulb. Indeed, it was the way the fish imagined heaven, much spookier and quieter than nature.

How they yearned for each other, these two, on such different levels.

The fish tried to imagine how the devil he could climb the string.

The Porcelain Figurine
The porcelain figurine grew waxen, her eyes grew glassy, shining as if alive, and with a sudden movement her arm dropped to her side, and timidly she turned her head to look around in wonderment. For years she had had her place upon the mantlepiece and now she tip-toed to its edge and gazed into the abyss of my living room — and then she turned to me

and in a tiny voice she said, "You . . . you must be Hans Christian Andersen!"

"No, I am not," I answered.

"Oh!" she sort of sadly said, and slowly retraced her steps to that place where she had stood, assumed her familiar pose, and has retained it to this day.

Where Is That Part of Me?

Where is that part of me that writes long elaborate stories, writes line after line? No doubt that "personality" thinks that it deserves a vacation in the Caribbean and has departed leaving me here for a while. Or perhaps it is in Canada eating bacon and eggs by candlelight while the Eskimos patiently wait for him and impatient huskies howl. Yet does he loll perhaps in India collecting prayer wheels and certain satins, green gauzes and yellow scarves ordinarily only treasured by primitive maidens and monks; now in some Himalayan hideaway he drinks dark tea surrounded by chests of ebony in which he keeps his collection of marbles, shining spheres of immortality; and does he not, though I be distant as in some dream, does he not ever think of me?

A Peculiar Greeting

"It is I, the rotten apple in the barrel, whose turn it is to fly and smash and splatter, thrown like a meteorite from the hand of a master — ah! I have caught your eye — I greet you!"

Blue

Three violet flowers nod in the breeze, busying bees, ballooning their violent color in an ultra-violet fog around their pistils, tapering to cobalt.

A turquoise insect appears on a twig.
It vanishes into the blue sky.
"Would you like an orange?"

Bloody Indigo

The clouds at sunset scream bloody indigo, and the fox pisses on the pumpkin. In the orchard there is a thief in every tree. The black cat loves the scarecrow more than you or I might imagine. For them every night is Halloween.

The Bloodthirsty Macaw

The bloodthirsty macaw that killed raccoons spoke Dutch.

The Sky Darkened With Greenery

The plants began to move, first withdrawing their roots from the soil, they began to writhe on the ground, pounding the earth with their leaves, bucking and jumping, and finally waving, like wings, their leaves, they flew, fluttering but a few feet at first, but soon the brown ground was bare, and the sky darkened with greenery.

The Hangman

The hangman turned and shot the prisoner whom he had been about to hang, and then he hanged himself.

A Kitchen in Time

Grinding of grain, hour before dawn, room full of red light flickering, jumping shadows of ovenlight, the clang of cast iron, the cook speaks Chinese to his helpers who have pigtails, great frying pans hang from the ceiling, a jar of huge spoons stands on the table, through the hush of night a distant gong beats three times, franz, franz, franz . . . one senses this scene is occurring in a different century, that these words are being translated from a foreign language . . . perhaps from the German, around 1920 possibly in Prague, in a crowded tiny restaurant with checkered tablecloths a bank clerk is scribbling this on his lunch hour.

The What-you-might-call Madness

The what-you-might-call madness of a man who survived ten days without food at the bottom of an abandoned well was that from then on he developed a passion for climbing trees.

Michigan Highway Mirage

A Michigan highway . . .

Tired of walking, clothing full of sweat, handkerchief sopping wet, shoes dusty, and thirsty, thirsty — yearning for a true *mirage.*

Yearning for palm trees, a vivid lake that will vanish, or the sea that really recedes, even as we approach it.

Up ahead a gas-station comes into view, and I hope the coca-cola will be cold . . . but what are those, moving into the driveway?

Camels. . . .

Sky-blue Shadows

The speck of white that is a sailboat and the one that is a gull . . .

The speck of black that is the vulture and one on the waves way out there . . . a porpoise, perhaps, leading a parade underwater . . .

It is 8 a.m.

A gibbous moon rests quietly, goes almost unnoticed, in the cloudless sky. The shadows of the mountains on the moon are sky-blue.

Freedom

"*Freedom* is spelled with seven letters," noticed the wise man, fondling his beard with his finger, thumbing its curls, while with his other hand he turned the pages of the Bhagavad Gita, and at that same moment that he said it, he opened the Book of Splendor, while with his other hand he made a note in pencil of a paragraph in the New Testament, while his other hand held up the Confucian Analects, and his other riffled the Koran, his other two hands are holding this book. He frowns.

"Bring me more light! Bring me my glasses!" he exclaims to a disciple, "I have only two eyes, and I can hardly believe what I see here!"

A Salt-water Fishtank

In the saloon in a great yacht, in an illuminated salt-water fishtank over the bar, there were fifty tropical fish, three scarlet squid, eight golden shrimp, and 48 snails.

In a furious storm, in which the ship floundered for five days, in the heart of the Pacific, it sank, a thousand miles from land, and it is said, and in a way it is true, in a sense, that there are no survivors.

Fire

Walking across the lawn in bare feet, otherwise rather nicely dressed for dinner, to turn around and see the building in flames, and to realize immediately that it is but a vision, understanding you must quickly leave this place you put on your shoes — and now to go in and face them all, old friends: to look into each face as if you had never seen it before, drunkenly making your adieus, probably we would think you weird, you who could receive the sign of our imminent doom.

Clouds of Orange

Clouds of orange dust rose into the air, and lightning shattered the sphere of summer silence with its thunder, smashing at the instant of the flame that tongued its way down the chimney filling the room with blazing death, utterly destroying the famous Oriental collection at the small museum deep in the suburbs of Chicago; and the fire would not be quenched by the downpour nor by Chicago firemen, but went on burning in the drizzle, so all that was standing was the ancient chimney — still smoking — when the Dalai Lama arrived.

Tell Us What the Tiger Fans Did *Then*!

"Tell us again, Grandpa. . . !" The retired baseball umpire sat deeper in his leather chair. The young boy continued, "How with the bases loaded in the ninth inning in the World Series the batter hit a line drive toward second base where you were standing and the ball hit you right between your arm and your chest and stuck there, and how your other hand just automatically reached over and plucked it from your armpit —"

King Midas

Her body flashes many bodies at me — lignum vitae, mercury, meerschaum, ice, jellyfish jade, banana-yellow cigaret smoke; she whispers hoarsely, "Think! — What would have happened had King Midas attained enlightenment? — Would that turn him into an ordinary human being?

"Or would the Universe turn into gold?"

Gumball
If you've never swallowed a gumball you won't know what I mean.

The Shoemaker
To be a shoemaker in a land where the people go predominantly barefoot is an art.

In Color
On moonless nights he walks over the oozy bog in snowshoes taking time-exposures in color of luminous mushrooms. It is the police chief's son.

Recognition
He found a folded-up foreign newspaper on the subway. He studied the front page trying to determine what language it was, but it was written in an unfamiliar alphabet. He was struck by the resemblance of someone pictured there to himself.

Memento
In a New England mansion after midnight, the great living room was lit by a few candles. Aware of distant voices, now alone in the room, now drunk, I sat on the floor clutching my glass.

As if having a race a gang of baby Galapagos tortoises came galloping across the floor towards me; each was as big as a hatbox, and bore in blazing letters branded on its carapace, the word "Memento".

The Sauce
The sauce was solid yellow ice, the fireplace was splattered, the cave cold, icicles hung from stalactites. A Neanderthal baby lay frozen in the arms of its mother, sprawled like a dancer since the days of the glaciers. Flashlights crisscrossed over the perfectly preserved bodies.

Lemon
He cut the lemon in half and found a hardboiled egg inside.

Warts
A hook-and-ladder truck screeched a warning horn, and the horse-drawn wagon of apples and watermelon barely escaped collision. In pulling sharply to a halt the wagon had swerved and a half-a-dozen apples fell onto the pavement right at the feet of a young boy who held a rope that was attached by a loop around the neck of a goat. The goat immediately began to eat one of the apples. The driver of the horse-and-wagon turned and stared at the goat eating the apple, and at the apples on the ground, and to the young boy he said thoughtfully, "I suppose it doesn't really matter, seeing as we're just characters in a story."

The boy said, "Imagine all my freckles turned into warts."

The Collector of Cymbals
He built his house over the elevator shaft of an abandoned salt mine, and in his house there was a small room whose only window was a trap door in the floor. He was a collector of cymbals, and whenever he got hold of a cymbal he would drop it down the shaft, and listen to it echo as it fell. He was a writer like me.

Objects of Mu

Objects of Mu, pearls of Ur in turquoise pools repose, while bold ghouls, six bald heads whose doctorates were on the dead, archaeologists, gaze fondly down on them, their "discovery" (six grins above the blue bowl) untouched beneath the temple for six thousand years, each still perfection of pale purity. On being popped into a felt cloth the finest pearl reflects — "How different were the smiles of the ancient kings."

Five Hundred Yellow Cabs

The intersection filled with yellow cabs.

The garage of the cab company was on fire and the news had flitted from taxi radio to radio and cabs came from all over the city out of curiosity and like bewildered insects whose nest had been destroyed they gathered and moved around the huge burning building, blocking the way of firetrucks, some vehicles abandoned in the middle of the street as drivers got out and gathered in groups to chat where they could get a better view, and as two floors collapsed with a tremendous crash and fire filled the windows with renewed fury and the black smoke of grease and gasoline put a plume into the stratosphere, the drivers began to blow their horns as cab drivers under stress have a wont to do, and that mourning music, such vibrant brass, of five hundred taxi drivers blowing their horns could be heard across the river.

The New

Winging past floods down into Ethiopia the stork disappeared over the horizon, while far below by a pyramid a Nile sparrow sang for a dying Pharaoh.

His tents were like flames on the desert sand.

Tethered white horses flashed in the sunlight.

Far below in the inner folds of the cloth palace a cricket

hailed the sparrow by his own song, and together they sang.

The wind joined them, playing the palms of the oasis, and the tentposts creaked, shifting from foot to foot as if tents thought of dancing this morning.

The new pyramid had already begun to practice its silence.